Walk Me Through the Darkness

Walk Me #3

Nicole Dennis

Blurb

Basil Wallstatt, former USMC sniper, is fighting to regain control of his body, emotions and life. After surviving a helicopter crash, he spent years in recovery. When he broke down and read the packet of letters from home, he knows its time to return to Montana. He needs to repair the broken bonds within his family. Even lost in the darkness of his past, he wonders if he can find the path back to the light.

Sound technician for Midnight Twang, Thomas Bellamy isn't on stage, but dresses with flash and style to cover the rest of the band. He's happy to be their 'peacock' and work in the ranch's kitchen instead of riding a horse. One of the first to see the mysterious newcomer, he can't believe he's looking upon his childhood crush that lasted through his life. With all of Basil's barriers, he's determine to not let him disappear again. He wasn't the only one who loves a Wallstatt sibling.

Warning: Past military experience, PTSD.

FatCat Books Ink

Trademarks

The author acknowledges the trademarked status and owners of the following word marks used in this story:

Ranger: *Polaris Industries, Inc.*

Stetson: *John B. Stetson Company*

Angry Birds: *Rovio Entertainment Corporation*

FaceTime: *Apple Inc.*

Noir: *Bath & Body Works for Men*

Chapter One

2 Years Earlier

As he did the same thing every morning since he woke up after the horrific helicopter crash that altered the course of his life and career in every imaginable way, USMC Sergeant Basil S. Wallstatt raised and lowered his lower right leg. Sweat poured down his face and back, soaking the ragged USMC sweatshirt with his efforts. His once matching thigh muscles flexed and moved under the tattered black gym shorts. Counting down the reps as he worked his leg through the stiffness, weakness, and pain against the machine, Bas did his best to push back the memories of the crash, of losing his best friend and lover, and his career.

Gritting his teeth, Bas went through five more reps and slowly lowered his leg to let the machine fall back in place. Picking up the towel, he wiped down his face and slung the cloth around his neck. He grabbed the waiting cane and shuffled to the next workout machine in the line. In this long-term rehabilitation and recovery center, he was supposed to work on both the physical and mental issues surrounding him since the crash and military career. Especially as one of the top-notched Marines Scout Sniper, the psychologists, psychiatrists, and counselors and all the others with the degrees were concerned about how he handled shooting bad guys when the order came down. He had no fucking problem shooting the bad guy, not if they were in the way or causing harm to his team. The only problem was the fucking helicopter coming down after a shot by an enemy sniper he somehow missed in the darkness.

Growling under his breath, Bas sat on the bench and twisted to set the correct weight. He tossed the towel and hated cane on the floor and spun into position.

"Hold up a moment, Basil," one of the counselors called out as he walked through the gym.

"In the middle of the therapy circuit, can't stop," Bas said, desperate to stall anything the man had to say to him.

"It's an order, soldier, put the bar down," the counselor said.

"Nice try pushing that button. I'm a Marine, not a soldier."

"At least I didn't call you a sailor."

Muttering a curse, Bas set the bar down and shifted to put his feet on the ground. He picked up the towel to dry some of the remaining sweat. "Anything I can help you with?"

His counselor and case manager, Daryl Franklin, held out a rubber-banded package of envelopes and waved them in front of Basil's face. He dropped on a bench opposite to face Basil. "How long are you going to ignore these letters?"

"I'm not interested in anything they have to say. They're from Montana. I have nothing back there."

"Your family lives there." Daryl waved the package again. "These are from your family."

"Don't have a family. Got kicked out when I came out and left for the Marines instead of following the path of all the other Wallstatts before me. Never looked back."

Daryl lowered his head and shook it. He tapped the package against his leg. "This is why we'll never break through anything we talk about in session. You have all these damn walls up and you refuse to drop them."

"My family has nothing to do with the helicopter crash. I missed a fucking sniper who shot the engine. That's the cause," Bas said, snapped the towel between them with his anger. He wrapped the towel around one of his hands, tightening it to feel his muscles respond. "I fucked up and missed the bastard. Five men are dead because of my fuck-up. I know exactly what happened. Case closed. Now I need to fix my body and get the hell on with my life." He released the towel and repeated the process.

"You want to get on with your life."

"That's the whole point I'm here. Right?"

"What happens when you leave this place? Will you add more silvery scars to your wrists? Hmm? Will you be in a grave this time instead of a hospital?"

"Low blow, doc. Low blow." Bas refused to look down at the thin silvery scars left crossing both of his inner wrists from a failed suicide attempt during his first stint in rehab.

"You don't stand in front of those walls and break them down. All you do is add another layer of plaster to cover the cracks and walk away. You've done the same thing since you left Montana."

"It's how I got through doing my job as a sniper. Everything in its compartment and not in the open. I concentrated on what I had to at the time to get the job done."

"Again with the deflection. If not walls, you deflect the questions."

Basil freed the towel from his hand and flicked it between them. "What the fuck do you want from me? I'm doing everything I'm supposed to around here. Yet, you keep fucking pushing me."

"That's my job!" Daryl snapped back at Basil. "I'm supposed to push you past all these fucking boundaries, lines, and deflections and force you to look at everything in your life. To break you down so you can rebuild yourself. That's what you're here to do. Not just rebuild your body, but your mind and soul as well. Otherwise, you will end up in a grave. I won't give you six months to live if you leave this place without working the way you're supposed too."

Basil straightened, surprised Daryl got his bad-assery up and in place. "Shit, didn't think you had that in you."

"I try not to let it show, but you're freaking impossible to play nice and charming with," Daryl said and muttered without heat, "Damn Marines."

"Not just a Marine, pal. A Scout Sniper." Sliding his finger into the neckline of his sweatshirt, Bas hooked the dog-tags out. He slid the tags to the side and held up a 7.62mm NATO bullet. "Have you ever seen another sniper with one of these?"

"What is it?"

"This is a bullet typically fired from the primary sniper rifle, a M40A3."

"What's the significance of having one of those bullets?"

"This is called a Hog's Tooth. It was presented to me after I graduated from Scout/Sniper School. According to military superstition, there is ultimately one round destined to end the life of each person, 'the round with your name on it.' Until that round is fired, the person for which it is intended is invincible. If the sniper carries this round at all times, it can never be fired and the sniper is therefore untouchable. It's been on this chain ever since and I was never hit by a round. Never."

"Fine, you're a sniper bad-ass."

"True, but if I'm invincible from a rifle shot, I don't want anything else to hit me."

"Including shots from your past and emotions."

"Exactly." Bas tucked the bullet and dog-tags back inside the sweatshirt. He may not be an active Marine any longer, but that didn't mean he would stop wearing his tags and tooth. "Since I graduated from Scout Sniper School, I haven't looked back. The walls were there to protect me and allow me to perform my duties as a Scout Sniper. I never failed. Not until that day."

"The day of the crash."

"I missed an enemy sniper and you know what happened. You have the damn file."

"Tell me anyway."

"We thought the job was done and returned to the helicopter for the flight back to base. It wasn't done. I missed a sniper in the shadows, he hid until we took off. The bastard shot out the engines of our helicopter and it went down. Men paid with their lives because of my fuck up."

"Do you think they would want you to live the rest of your life blaming yourself? To never live for yourself and them?"

Bas didn't answer. The face of his fellow teammate, spotter, and best friend appeared before his face. Going against all the rules, they fell in love with one another and became lovers. Keeping their relationship under the radar and behind the roles of best friends, he never felt alone and abandoned. When Lieutenant Lawrence "Larry" Corbin was by his side with his crazy attitude and wild grin, things got better. Even when they were deep in shit, he counted on Larry to keep things together and let their attitude and determination disappear.

Stretching out his right leg, Bas dug the heel of his hand into the upper muscle group. He stared down at the destruction of his leg caused by numerous deep second-degree and third-degree burns, surgeries to reconnect all the bones, and multiple skin grafts. The burns covered most of his lower back, hips, and upper legs. Some kind of miracle had him curl into a fetal position that spared his groin and inner legs from the damage. While he healed the multiple fractures in his ribs, pelvis, and legs, the issues from the compression fractures in his spine and the burns took longer. Even three years out from the accident, he required several rounds of skin grafts along a particular section of his lower back destroyed from a deep third-degree burn. Since the third-degree burns destroyed everything through the muscle, he didn't feel pain. It was the flash second-degree burns sending out all kinds of shit. Those suckers caused the most pain and often required the doctors to knock him out with heavy anesthetics before performing any kind of cleaning or re-dressing.

The shiny twisted skin and webs of scars on his body would forever remind him of the fatal crash. The crash took Larry's life right in front of him. He never forgot how Larry's brilliant green eyes faded in front of him as he gasped his last breaths. He was helpless to save Larry as he was with the rest of the members of the team.

"Why the hell was I the one to survive?" Bas kept his tone low and soft.

"No one, not even you, will ever be able to answer the question. All you can do is concentrate on making the most of this second chance at life," Daryl said. "It starts with facing everything you have hidden inside you. To man up and face your fears, the walls, and the cracks. That's your job." He held out the envelopes. "You can start your journey with these gifts."

"Gifts?"

"A token from home to try anew. They're pieces of paper. They can't hurt."

"The words on them can shred you apart."

"Let them. They'll show you the way."

Letting out a heavy sigh, knowing he couldn't run any further, Basil accepted the package.

"Go outside and read them. It's a nice day and you should enjoy it. I'll be in my office when you're done. Find me when you're ready to talk about strategy."

Basil picked up his cane and limped to the double glass doors.

"Bas..."

Looking over his shoulder, Basil met Daryl's gaze.

"This is the first step. It's the hardest, but I know you can do it."

Swallowing at the truth and promise in Daryl's words, Basil stepped outside to start the journey of healing.

Chapter Two

Current Time

Thanking the driver for the ride, Basil stood at the end of the long road winding through the Triple W property. He had all of his worldly belongings with him plus an extra four-legged addition in the form of an energetic black Labrador/Schnauzer mix three-year old who went by the name of Stryker. While Bas stared at the weathered fences and road, he could also follow Stryker's movements as the pup sniffed out all the different scents and even marked a few places. Life on the streets of Baltimore and a year in the shelter didn't give Stryker much of a beginning, but Bas made sure the pup had one since their gazes met.

The quiet motor of a Ranger utility vehicle drew closer.

"*Holy shit*, I don't believe this," someone drawled out as the motor dropped to a low rumble.

Turning his head, Basil saw the utility vehicle sitting on the other side of the fence a few feet up the road. A cowboy sat behind the wheel, a box of tools set on the bed behind the two-seater. The cowboy pushed back the once-white Stetson and leaned forward, crossing arms over the steering wheel.

Narrowing his gaze against the sun, Bas reached behind him to the simplified tactical backpack hanging on his good shoulder. Unzipping one of the pockets, he yanked out a utility cover in desert camo. Tugging it into place to give his face some shade, he zipped the pack. Whistling to Stryker, he hefted the large green canvas sea bag that he stuffed with his life's possessions and slung it over his back. He filled the backpack with his immediate and personal shit he wanted close by during traveling. It took a flight, a bus ride and then the truck ride to get his ass to this point. His body was killing him. Not giving a shit about revealing his disabilities, he plugged the cane into the ground and moved his body up the road. It took a few slow limping steps until his legs and back loosened enough.

Stryker danced around his feet before bounding over to the Ranger. He wiggled under the lowest rung of the fence and sniffed all around, doing what dogs do best when seeing something new.

A little slower, Basil stopped at the fence line. He dropped the sea bag to the ground and leaned against the fence, breathing harder than he liked at the simple short walk.

"Basil Wallstatt. Where the hell have you come from?" the cowboy asked as he left the Ranger and walked around to meet Basil face-to-face. He paused to say hello to the wiggling pup and made his way to the fence.

At that point, Basil recognized one of his cousins, the oldest of three brothers who worked the cattle ranch on the far side of Triple W. "Hello, Randall. Long time no see." Basil held out his hand.

"Aww... Shit, we're family, you goofball," Randall Wallstatt said, as he grasped Basil's hand, tugged it between them as he leaned over the fence to wrap his other hand around Basil's back. He thumped his upper back a few times with the manly hug.

"Easy. Easy there, please," Basil said. "It's good to see you too."

"Shit. Sorry, man. Why are you so damn stiff?" Randall asked, pulling back.

"Bad ride on a chopper."

Fixing the Stetson, Randall winced at Basil's simple answer.

To clear the awkwardness, Basil changed the subject. "How's Uncle Liam and Aunt Jenny?"

"They're doing good, worried about your mama, but holding up. Ranch is doing fine. Everyone is fine. Enough with the shit talk."

Randall adjusted his Stetson and stared at his older cousin. "What are you doing here?"

Adjusting the cover to fit better, Bas stared at the ground and then at his cousin. "Charlie. He's been writing to me since I left, filling me in on what's happening around here. Though, I've been a wuss about reading and answering them."

"He told you about your mama."

Basil nodded. "What's the news about her?"

"She's hanging in there. Your mama is one helluva strong woman. The docs are surprised she's hanging in there, but they're keeping her comfortable."

"Docs?"

"Hmm. Doc Alfred Sampson asked his nephew, Doc Evan Sampson, to join the practice. Doc Evan fell for our fiddle player and is bunking here with him."

About to say something, Bas held up a hand as he went back through the pronouns. "Gay. A gay couple is living together on the ranch?"

"Sure. They're not the only ones. Sage is still here with his fella, Kaden Carmody."

"One of the Carmody kids from the Double C."

"That's the kid," Randall said. "Thought you said Charlie wrote you."

"He mentioned Sage fell in love and was happy."

"That sly dog was covering shit up to get you here."

"Probably..." Bas gripped the fence.

Gay. Men could be out and proud and work the Triple W. How the hell is that possible?

"When Sage came out to your daddy, everything changed around here. Your daddy bellowed at you something awful and acted like a grumpy ass grizzly bear, but when Sage spoke to him, he turned into a teddy bear. It was a shock to everyone. He even supported the news when Sage started a country-rock band, bringing in me, my brothers, and some of the cowboys. Hell, he turned the old barn into a studio and practice area."

"I bet it was. I knew Sage would follow his dream to play music. What's the band's name?"

"It's called Midnight Twang. We might even get a record deal soon. We're on hiatus since our fiddle player has some recovering to do and the situation with your mama."

Bas thumped the cane once in the dirt and looked out over the land he grew up on and left behind. *So many changes...*

"Anyway, having Doc Evan stay on the ranch is giving everyone some extra relief that if anything happens, he'll be around to help. Come on. Let's get you up to the ranch. Everyone will wanna see you." Done talking for the moment, Randall grasped hold of the sea bag and hefted it over his shoulder. "Holy shit, man, what the hell is in this thing?"

"My life," Basil said as he studied how to get through the fence. First, he stuffed the backpack through the fence. Then he carefully made his way through the cross-posts without messing up his body any further. Slinging the backpack over one shoulder, he stepped to the Ranger.

"Are you home for good?"

"As long as everyone wants me around, yup, I'm tired of carrying my life in a bag."

"I hear you, buddy. Nothing is like putting your roots down. You're the only missing piece of the family, Bas. Always have been," Randall said as he set the sea bag in the back. He added Basil's backpack next to it. He climbed into the driver's seat. "Where does your pup wanna sit?"

"He's still on the small side thanks to the Schnauzer blood and can sit on the floor with me," Basil said and whistled to the pup.

Circling around the long way, Stryker ran over to them. He jumped into the Ranger and settled between Basil's legs on the floor. His butt wiggled with the force of his tail.

"Ssh. Easy, bud," Bas said as he rubbed the pup's soft ears.

Stryker rested his muzzle on Bas's knee for the ride.

As Randall drove around the circular walkway, Basil took in everything from the changes in the main house, the additional vehicles parked to the side, and a massive bus with the name Midnight Twang scrolled across the side. Letting Stryker out first, Basil planted the cane in place and stepped out. He reached back and gathered the heavy backpack, dragging it up to one shoulder. He reached for the sea bag, but Randall waved him off.

Randall whistled hard and shrill.

"What was that?"

"Simple alert. Everyone else is working on the range or the different corrals. We got a new herd of Mustangs to break and train which is keeping everyone busy along with the regular stuff."

"Why are you here and not at your daddy's place?"

"Daddy has enough men to cover us and we put time in there. My younger brothers are home with him. I'm here to help Sage and Charlie. Since we got back from the tour with a busted fiddle player, the news of your mama and basic stuff around here, Sage has been stressing. I think Kaden took him for a long ride."

"Did they go to his cave?"

Randall glanced over at him. "How do you know about the cave?"

"Please, I found my way there once or twice. Did they go to the cave?"

"Probably. They haven't been there in a while."

"I can't believe that place is still there. Thought someone would forget about it or the mountain would hide the entrance somehow."

"Nope, it's still there and I think they fixed it up over the years. If it was closer, I'm sure those two would build a house."

Rubbing a hand over the back of his neck, Basil checked out the expanded and freshly painted house. "They added an extra wing."

"The kitchen, pantry and dining room increased and turned all gourmet. I don't know. All I know is Lorraine was beaming. Above is a new master suite for Sage and Kaden. They arranged the extra rooms and bathrooms into suites along with a little adjustment on the lower area. Only thing that didn't move was the entrance, family room and your daddy's office. The rest updated as needed over time. We gave the outside a fresh coat of paint last year."

Walking past the house, he turned and found the old barn, also freshly painted, and a larger barn behind and to the side. Several corrals were in between them. To another side he saw two stretched out buildings near one another and pointed to them in a silent question.

"Those are the new bunkhouses. Sage changed the design from the typical large room of bunks to smaller rooms for everyone's privacy."

"Has this place expanded so much we could afford all this? Has there been some trouble? I couldn't respond or come here any sooner than what I have."

"On a mission?"

"Hospital bed and multiple rehabilitation centers," Basil admitted.

"Shit."

"As I said earlier, it was a bad crash. The kind most don't walk away from and I almost didn't."

"Shit, man," Randall said, drawing out the words.

"I'm getting beyond it, but I feel like I fucked up by not being able to help."

"Kaden helped out. He cleaned things up with the bank, got them off Sage's ass and helped Sage and Charlie. They turned this place around. With the addition of mustang blood to the quarter horses, we're closer to your daddy's dream of a good mix breed horse. There's a waiting list several years out for ranches and cowboys wanting one of the colts or fillies. A lot are also from the rodeo circuits."

"Had a feeling Sage would do better around here than me."

"He's doing his best, Charlie and Kaden support him along with the rest of the guys," Randall said.

"Now I need to figure out how to fit back in the mix. It's a little difficult for me to get on a horse in my condition. I'm not as flexible or agile."

"You're family. They'll welcome you no matter how you come." Randall patted his hand on Basil's back and pointed back to the house.

Turning, Basil moved his gaze along the wrap-around porch. He saw an older couple stepping out from one of the side doors and recognized them in an instant. Triple W would be nothing without their presence and lives given to this land.

He walked-limped to the closest stairs and climbed them. He dropped his backpack, whipped off his cap, and wrapped his arms around his second mother, Lorraine Wyght. His cane clambered to the porch, but he didn't care. He breathed in the warm scents of cinnamon, flour, and coffee clinging to Lorraine and knew he was home. He closed his eyes as Lorraine hugged him tight, though she barely reached his upper chest. As the embrace continued, he pressed a kiss to the top of her graying-brown hair swept back in a simple bun.

Looking over Lorraine's head, Basil stared at his father's right-hand man, who helped build Triple W and kept her going with Sage, Charlie Wyght. Like Lorraine, Basil looked upon Charlie as a second father. It was Charlie's persistence and belief in him that brought him back to the ranch. Freeing his arm from Lorraine, he held it out to Charlie.

Taking his hand, Charlie stepped into Basil's embrace, sharing it with his wife. Charlie lifted his work-roughened hand and pressed it against the back of Basil's head, tugging him closer to the embrace.

"Welcome home, boy," Charlie said.

Basil couldn't hold it back. He wept in their arms.

With his belly full of Lorraine's awesome down-home cooking, Basil and Charlie moved to the living room to discuss everything. The first thing they did was place a call to his sister, Rosemary, to let her know he returned home. For the first five minutes, he heard nothing but pure squealing and gushing from Rose. With their mama's precarious health, Rose said she would bring the family up for a visit after Sage returned from the cave with Kaden. She mentioned how they needed to sit down and talk about things and Basil agreed.

After the call, they dove into the deeper things, which a simple letter couldn't convey. There was far too many years for them to cover. They started from when he left the ranch, briefed over Basil's military career, touched on the accident, and concentrated on the ranch. Charlie left once to find something in the office behind the large living room. He returned with several folders and laptop.

As Lorraine brought over coffee and dessert, they hunched over the coffee table. Well, Charlie hunched over while Basil remained rather straight due to his messed-up body.

"I'm impressed you fellas are using an actual computer to enter the books and not Daddy's old fashioned leather-bound ledgers," Basil said as he clicked into the accounting program and opened several years' worth of financial reports.

"When Kaden came on board, he insisted on purchasing the darn thing and all the software. We can track everything from daily expenses to the lineage of all the horses. There's even a calendar to follow all the breeding mares and their cycles. There are reports on each foal's birth, training, qualities, and potential buyers. Instead of working never ending days on the books, the boys can finish in a few hours, using information from the others to gather all the numbers and updates," Charlie said.

When he slid a folder closer, Charlie flipped it open to turn some pages toward Basil. "These reports start ten years ago. The first five show the decline in all the figures. We were barely making ends meet, but I didn't know Sage channeled the money for the mortgage payments into salaries for the hands, feed for the horses, and other items."

"He was still dealing with high school," Bas said.

"His last two years were rough on him. The shining light was the band. It got better when Kaden reappeared and they got over the rough patches." Charlie looked around them to make sure they were alone. "Kaden gave me this folder in private. He found these amongst his father's papers when he and his lawyer moved the ranch business to a new manager after the elder Carmody's arrest."

"Arrest?"

"There were multiple charges on both the state and federal levels. He's stuck behind a cage in a federal penitentiary. The man was lower than scum. Kaden bore the brunt of it for most of his life."

While he picked up the pages, Basil stretched and moved his back to straighten out the building kinks. The paper was thick letterhead of the Double C. He stared at letters the elder Carmody wrote to outside buyers. The man came close to outright blackballing the horses from Triple W, saying they were inferior and wild with no stamina or worth. A couple more exchanges between the Double C and the local bank his daddy did business with for decades. Carmody and some of the top bank folks worked together to try and destroy the Triple W in order for Carmody to absorb the land into the Double C for a mere fraction.

"That lousy sonofabitch," Basil said as he tossed the letters on the table. "Why the hell would he target us?"

"It was a feud that went back to when your father and Carmody were in school."

"Sage almost paid the ultimate price. I should have—"

"Don't go there. The bank told us they sent you a certified letter about the eminent foreclosure and demand of payment. Here's a copy," Charlie said as he held out another page.

Basil lifted his head to search the room. "Where's my backpack?"

"We placed your things at the back of the room. I wasn't sure where you wanted to sleep. I'll get it," Charlie said as he pushed up and headed to a corner. He returned with the large backpack.

"Thanks," Basil said as he set the pack on the floor and unzipped one of the large pockets. He pulled out a packet of envelopes and unwrapped the rubber band. He flipped through the envelopes, muttering dates as he checked them, and kept shaking his head. "I never received a letter. These were all the letters gathered while I was at Walter Reed. It's not here."

"Another lie on their part."

"It's too late to do something." Basil tossed the stack of envelopes aside. "How did Kaden help straighten things out?"

Charlie explained everything about Kaden's inheritance and handling the bank. "Triple W no longer has a mortgage and is debt-free. Kaden refuses to be paid back, saying this is his home and he helped keep it that way."

"He's a damn good kid."

"Sure is. Your little brother is knocked stupid by him."

"Randall mentioned they were at the cave."

"It's been their special place since they were kids. Sage has been on edge since your mama's diagnosis. Plus there was Josh's accident and surgeries on top of the issue. Things became overwhelming and he suffered from severe anxiety attacks. Kaden had enough and said he was taking them out of here. He packed their things, saddled their horses, and took Sage to the cave yesterday. I don't expect them back for a couple of days."

"What should I do until then?"

"Walk around the place. Get back in touch with your family's land," Charlie said and paused. "You should see your mother."

"From what I read, she wouldn't know I'm there."

"Still, you should look in on her at the old cabin."

"I'll do that in the morning."

"Be sure to visit your daddy's grave, son. You need to come to terms with him. He's with the rest of the Wallstatt clan under the twin oaks. I'll make sure a Ranger is available for you for both trips."

"Yes, sir. I was planning on that before I talk to Sage. Until I correct things with Daddy, I'm not going to feel like I belong home."

"Good. You need to talk things through to him. Once he got over his anger and Sage coming out, he missed you more than you could imagine. Both of you were too damn stubborn to take the first step."

"It's why we keep you around, Charlie."

Charlie snorted and waved the thought away. "Once you see your mama and talk to your daddy, take it easy for a bit. Sage should be back by then. The hard work will come later. All right?"

Basil nodded and hugged the older man. "I need to get up and move or I'm going to regret it." He grasped his cane and used it to pull himself to his feet.

Off to the side, Stryker awoke from his light doggy nap and got to his paws.

With his head filled after his discussion with Charlie, Basil stepped outside onto the porch. Stryker followed at his heels. He went to the railing, rested a hand upon the stop, and stared out over the ranch. The sun long since set in the western sky, the colorful sky deepening to a velvet midnight blue filled with stars and a crescent moon.

While he talked with Charlie, he knew life on the ranch continued in an ordered pattern. The cowboys finished their work for the day, brought in and cared for their horses as they chatted about whatever happened or plans for later. He heard when they gathered around the extended kitchen table filled with Lorraine's good cooking, but didn't join them.

He needed to see Sage first. Perhaps his brother and...*holy shit*...and his partner would return soon from their mountain trip.

His little brother was something else. Basil shook his head with a smile. Thanks to all the shit he went through with their father, he was happy to learn Sage had a smoother ride when he came out. Sage got the chance to grow up on this land, figure out who he was, and fall in love with his childhood best friend.

Thanks to recent decision by the Supreme Court, he wondered if this old ranch would see another wedding. The last one was his sister's to her beloved cop, which he missed and regretted to this day. He heard he was an uncle, but never met her children.

Dragging fingers through his hair that grew longer since he left the rehab center, Basil pulled in a deep cleansing breath of pure Montana air. He closed his eyes as he listened to the stillness, the neighing and whinnying of horses talking to one another, and knew he was home.

"Home," he repeated aloud.

After tapping his fingers on the railing, he returned inside, gathered his belongings, and found his way to one of the back rooms. He didn't want to choose a final room to move into tonight. Not until he spoke with his daddy's grave and Sage. He wouldn't blame Sage if he kicked him right back on the streets for deserting the family. Until they talked, Basil wouldn't overstep boundaries.

Settling into the room, he went through his evening stretches and therapy. After a quick shower, he sat and wrote in his journal until it was time to shut off the lights. Once he committed all of his attention to recovery, he learned different techniques to calm his mind with Daryl. One was simply to put pen to paper and write everything down. He filled several journals since he started and had no plans on stopping. Not even time could heal his issues, only hard work for the rest of his life. He could do the work. Every day of his life.

Chapter Three

Useless out on the ranch with his slender frame and hands, Thomas made himself available to help to Lorraine and Charlie closer to the house and bunkhouses. Both of them were getting up in age, not that either one would ever acknowledge the fact. He figured they deserved a younger pair of hands and back.

Instead of the typical cowboy outfit of broken-in boots, faded jeans, and a plaid shirt of some kind, Thomas dressed a little different. Okay, a lot different, not that he gave a shit what anyone thought. Full of colors and styles, he played with his clothes. He was more flamboyant than the rest of the band and proud of being the group's 'peacock.' At first, he smacked the hell out of the Wallstatt cousins for giving him that name, but then he strutted around and owned it. Hell yes, he liked being called such a beautiful bird. He would kill for that kind of plumage. For the last five years, he turned up his style.

Today he paired slim-fitting dark wash jeans with a sky-blue shirt and fake snakeskin boots. He jazzed up his hair with a bit of gel. Instead of the usual thin metal-frame glasses, he selected a blue plastic frame to match the shirt. A feathered owl charm pendant necklace finished the outfit to perfection. He slicked his lips with his beloved lip balm, this time in a sweet mint flavor. As he tucked the stick in the front pocket of his jeans, he left his room.

Thomas didn't see Lorraine in the kitchen, which was unusual. She normally beat him into the kitchen by several hours. Same with Charlie. Both were o-dark-clock morning birds and punctual as hell.

"Lorraine?" Thomas called out, but didn't get a reply.

Thanks to watching and helping Lorraine for years, he became pretty adept and skilled in the kitchen. While he hummed a tune, he tugged on the rainbow apron Lorraine gave him as a Christmas present and tied it around his waist. He washed his hands at the sink, dried, and tucked the towel into the apron pocket. He had the large coffee maker brewing the precious java. Once the caffeine started bubbling, he checked out the daily menus written on the large white-board near the fridge.

"First up is a Southwest Oven-Baked Omelet Casserole. I can do that," Thomas said as he flipped the pages in the binder they kept next to the board. He clicked open the rings and selected the plastic covered recipe. Closing the binder, he carried the page to the longer prep counter and went through it. "Sweet, it bakes in the oven and I don't have to babysit it. Yay. Time for the good stuff," he said and headed to the fridge. He tugged out the fixings from the carton of eggs to different vegetables and milk. He left those on the counter and went to the pantry for more ingredients. The last ones he found in the spice cabinet.

Once he laid everything out in order of the recipe, he ran his finger down the steps. He cleaned, chopped, and diced his way through the onions, peppers, garlic, and a couple of green chilies. He clicked the heat under the cast-iron skillet and swirled some oil. Within a few moments, he sautéed the filling, adding drained cans of sweet corn and black beans, until everything was golden and softened.

While the filling finished, he cracked and whisked the egg mixture, finished with the spices and folded in the sautéed vegetables. He split the mixture between the glass baking dishes and topped everything with a grated cheese blend. When the oven dinged, he slid both dishes inside and set the timer for an hour.

A quick cleanup and he was on to the next dish. Thanks to all the cowboys, he knew it would include bacon somewhere. Another check on the board told him to create the corned beef and bacon hash.

"Yup, knew there would be bacon," he said while he followed the previous steps.

As he slid the prepared dish into the second oven, the coffee maker dinged. He poured a large mug, lightened it with cream, and savored the first few sips.

"Morning, Thomas, I apologize for my delay." Lorraine walked into the kitchen. She tugged on her apron that said '*Don't Mess with the Chef*' and washed her hands. "Oh wow, you did so much. Thank you."

"Morning, coffee is ready. I saw the casserole took a little longer to bake so I figured to start it right away. The hash is in the second oven and I was going to slice up the fruit."

"Do you even need me in here?" She poured a mug of coffee, doctored it how she wanted, and sipped it.

"Of course. No one can make your fluffy buttermilk biscuits. Mine become pitiful hockey pucks."

Lorraine chuckled. "It's all in how you work the dough."

"So you keep telling me."

"What else do we need today?" She ran her finger down the board. "Hmm. Potatoes, sausage and bacon are in the hash. The omelet covers the eggs and vegetables. Biscuits and fresh fruit should do it."

Thomas smiled behind his mug as Lorraine checked over everything. She maintained a well-balanced meal throughout the day for everyone to enjoy. She was proud of the meals turned out and Thomas pleased to assist her in feeding the crew.

They worked together the rest of the morning on the remaining pieces. Once finished on his end, he gathered the plates, utensils, glasses, and mugs and stacked everything on the sidebar for everyone to grab as they went through the line. Over time, they discovered it was easier to set everything up by buffet and eat at the table, especially after the expansion of the area. He set up the hot plates and transferred the casserole dishes to two of them. After a quick slicing job, he covered them with foil to keep warm.

"Can you get the bag of green onions, sour cream and salsa from the outer fridge? We need them to top off the casserole. I need to finish cutting these biscuits."

"Sure," Thomas said and left the attached dining room that flowed directly from the kitchen. He loved how the remodel made mealtimes a whole lot easier to maneuver.

When he returned with his arms full, he stopped short. A tall male figure walked out the opposite doorway, carrying a tray. Dressed in camouflage pants and gray T-shirt, the man wasn't dressed like anyone else on the ranch.

Entering the kitchen, he unloaded the items onto the counter. "Who was that?"

Lorraine jumped in surprise and pressed a hand to her chest. "Thomas, dear, you scared me."

"Lorraine?"

"Someone you'll meet soon, but not yet."

At the cryptic answer, Thomas looked at the doorway and back to the lady he loved more than his mother, who turned away from him. With a shrug, knowing he couldn't push Lorraine to answer anything she didn't want, he sliced through the scallions and dished up the cream and salsa. He organized them next to the casserole dishes for the guys to top as they choose.

Finishing up with the coffee and juice options, he watched as Lorraine stepped onto the porch and rang the loud bells to call everyone to the kitchen. It was the start to a long day.

Other than the one morning when he visited the old cabin to peek in on his mother, Basil didn't feel like leaving the ranch house the rest of the time. This one felt different. Basil woke up with the intention of leaving the ranch house. He dressed in soft loose jeans and a Marine T-shirt and dark canvas slip on shoes. He picked up a small daypack and tucked his sunglasses, desert camo utility cover, wallet and phone inside, steadied himself on the cane and whistled to Stryker as they headed to the kitchen.

Same as the other mornings, he caught sight of the brightly dressed male helping Lorraine. He checked out the coffee dark hair, styled long on the top, and the slim body outlined in the clothes that were definitely not your typical cowboy fare. This morning, the man was in dark wash jeans and a purple plaid shirt. He danced and worked with Lorraine as a choreographed team.

Since he didn't want anyone to know he was around until he spoke with Sage, he waited until the man left the kitchen. He entered from the opposite side and knocked on the door.

"Good morning," Lorraine said as she stepped over and kissed his cheek. She cooed to Stryker, who barked in answered. "I set up Stryker's meal around the corner."

"Go on, boy, go find breakfast," Basil said to the dog.

With another bark, Stryker pranced away, tail wagged the entire time.

"Such a happy pup," Lorraine said. "Do you want to sit with us for breakfast?"

"Not until Sage and I talk, please."

"And your mother?"

"I went to the cabin a couple of mornings ago and peeked inside. I heard her arguing and left."

"If you insist on this foolish notion to wait for your brother, very well, though I think it's silly. What do you want for breakfast?"

"Could I have a small thermos of my tea and a couple of sandwiches?" Basil held up the daypack. "I'm going to the twin oaks."

"Are you sure you want to go alone?"

"I need too. Stryker will be with me."

"What if you—"

"I'll have my phone."

"It doesn't always work out here. Stop and see Charlie for a radio." She walked off to finish his tea and transferred it to a thermos. She filled a pair of fresh biscuits with the egg mixture. In a couple of others, she piled in bacon and the hash mixture. Once she wrapped everything and closed the thermos, she carried everything back to him.

Basil opened the pack and helped her situate everything inside.

"One more thing." She pulled a bottle of water from the fridge to add to the pack. "In this weather, hydration is the key. Is the weight okay?"

"It'll be okay. I'm going to take a Ranger." He locked the drawstring and slung it over one shoulder.

"I'm back, Lorraine," the young man called out as he entered the opposite side, but didn't look up to find them talking.

"Who is that?" Basil whispered. "He's rather adorable."

Lorraine looked over her shoulder at her assistant and back to Basil. "Do you like the way he looks?"

"My body may be a little banged up, Lorraine, but doesn't mean I'm dead."

"Don't go telling an old lady such stuff." She looked over her shoulder with a secretive grin. "Don't you recognize him?"

Basil shook his head.

"Think about it. It'll come to you. If he's not here helping me for the meals, you'll find him in the music barn."

"I plan on checking that out later."

"You'll see him there." With that mysterious answer, she left him standing there without a full answer.

"But..." Basil let the protest die out.

Stryker nudged his leg with his head and let out a soft whine.

Basil glanced down at the pup that licked his chops. "Enjoy your breakfast?"

Stryker wagged his tail and let out a low burp.

"Pleasant," Basil said with a roll of his eyes at the dog's manners.

"What was that?"

It was the same male voice from earlier.

Basil glared down at his dog.

Stryker dropped his head down and covered his nose with both paws.

"Yeah, sure you're sorry," he said in a low tone without any heat in it. "Come on, you furry brat. We have things to do today."

After another check of the attractive male, Basil hummed in pleasure. He walked away and headed outside. In the closest barn, he found Charlie and Randall talking. Charlie saw him first.

"Morning, Basil, how are you?" Charlie asked.

"Up and moving, sir, which is the best I can hope for at this time. I'm hoping to take you up on the offer of the Ranger again this morning. This time, Lorraine told me to ask for a radio since my phone may not work."

"Gonna go to the twin oaks?"

"Yes, sir, I am," Basil said.

"Good for you. It's the right thing. Randall, can you take Basil to my Ranger? Show him how it works and give him an extra radio," Charlie said. "I'll be around if you need to talk about anything later."

"Thank you, sir."

Randall led Basil and Stryker away. "How are you holding up?"

"Wishing I could speak with Sage to feel more sure-footed about being here," Basil said, "but I need to talk to my daddy first. Everything started back with him. I checked in on Mama, but couldn't talk to my aunt. Figured it's best I man up and talk to my daddy."

"I wish you luck and offer my support." Randall gave Basil's upper arm a light squeeze. He stopped at the barn to grab a set of keys and a radio. "Okay. Driving a Ranger is pretty damn easy. Just gotta watch over the dips and holes. It could send you rocking out of the seat." He gave him a quick rundown on how to operate the utility vehicle.

Basil placed the daypack on the seat and called Stryker to hop up. Once he got used to the mechanisms, he nodded his thanks. He pulled the sunglass out of the pack and slid them up his nose. He tugged out the utility cover next and tugged it down over his head.

Randall flicked the floppy edge with his fingers. "Do we need to get you a proper Stetson to replace this flopping thing?"

"I've worn this for about as long as I wore a Stetson. I'm used to it."

"It looks ridiculous out here. We need to take you into town and get a properly fitted Stetson." Randall glanced down at the shoes and huffed. "And a pair of boots."

"I can't do the boots. There's not much flexibility below my waist."

Randall waved his hand below Basil's waist. "What about below the belt? Are you..."

"All intact? Yes."

"That's a positive outlook on life. Can't move for crap, but you still have your cock. You're all set."

Basil laughed at his cousin's take on his injuries.

Randall backed away from the Ranger. "She's all yours. Any issues, give a holler." He held out the radio which Basil took in hand. "The radio is set on our station. Just hit the button and call out. Someone will get back to you. It also has a GPS unit so we'll find you."

Basil dropped the radio in the holder on the dash. "Thanks. Hopefully there will be none."

With a rev of the engine, Basil pushed down on the gas pedal and steered north toward the looming mountains. He would follow the similar path to where Sage was staying with Kaden in their hidden cavern system, but go further west to find the twin oaks that entwined over the years and guarded over the Wallstatt family plot for generations.

Less than a half hour later, he saw the twin oaks rise above the ground. He parked near the gate and turned off the engine. He leaned forward and folded his arms over the steering wheel.

In front of him rested a simple plot of twenty graves ranging in ages with room for more. The entire plot was surrounded by a double layer of iron fences to protect it from wildlife. The twin oaks loomed over the entire plot, guarding it under the shadow of the canopy. Though it hurt his heart to think about it, they would add a new grave within the year.

With a long sigh, Basil leaned back in the seat and dug into the pack. He unwrapped a sandwich and ate it in a few quick bites. He followed it with several sips of the honey-laced herbal tea Daryl swore helped with healing. All Basil craved was a strong cup of coffee.

Since he couldn't put it off any longer, he twisted the top back on the thermos and set it in the holder. He pulled off the hat and tossed it on the pack. With the cane in one hand, he climbed out of the Ranger. Stryker hopped out and raced around the area.

"Stay close, buddy. Go do your business somewhere," he said to the pup.

Stryker rolled in the sun-warmed grass. It was good to be a dog.

He couldn't say the same for himself. There were much deeper things in his life.

He moved with his awkward step-limp gait until he reached the gate. He lifted the gate's latch and swung it open. He swept his gaze over the graves. He headed to some of the older ones, swept off some debris from the natural granite stones, and did a painful bend over to pluck the annoying weeds.

On the newer side, he touched the twin graves of his uncles and their wives, a couple of cousins who passed far too soon, a pair of stillborn siblings his mother mourned, and finally stopped at the last one. His father. The name of Niall Lafayette Wallstatt engraved in the shiny granite face and colored with a touch of black. Underneath the days, his mother added 'Loving Brother, Husband and Father - Taken too soon from the land he loved.'

After reaching out to clean the stone, Basil groaned as he lowered himself to the ground to the left side of the grave. He plucked and tossed aside some of those pesky weeds. A wilted bouquet of Montana's natural wildflowers rested against the base. He touched his fingers to the petals as he recognized the tawny daylily, a couple types of evening primroses, asters, and daisy varieties. These were all flowers that grew naturally around their lands. Someone was here within the last few days to leave the bouquet.

Basil traced his father's name. He cleared his throat and pulled off his glasses.

"Hi, Daddy, I came home," he said as he placed his hand flat on the stone. "I'm home. We need to discuss some things."

Chapter Four

Steadier after the visit to his father's grave and the quiet conversation, Basil felt some weight lifted from his shoulders. Some more would be gone when he saw his brother. The rest...well...the rest would be when he could face, truly face, what happened to Larry. That piece would take some time. He didn't know how long and couldn't push it.

He took advantage of the quieting of the internal storm a couple of days later by relaxing in the rocking chair. While he rocked, he lifted his head and breathed in the fresh air, catching some additional scents from the horses and cowboys who worked the land. He stared at the setting sun filled the sky in an array of colors. The peacefulness of the late afternoon became interrupted when he heard something. He stopped the rocker and raised an eyebrow.

"What is that, boy?" he asked Stryker, who didn't budge from his nap.

Music? Rock music?

Moving down the stairs, Basil whistled to alert Stryker. The pup scrambled to his paws and trotted after him. Bas made his careful way across the grounds and to the old barn his father turned into a music studio. Something he still couldn't believe would ever happen, but Charlie swears it was the truth. Over the last couple of days, this was the one place he didn't inspect like everything else. This place belonged to Sage, but now the music intrigued and called to him.

Pushing open one door, he entered the vast reformed space. His jaw about hit the floor. On the far side was a good size stage, filled with instruments and equipment. There was special padding and material to help boost and contain the sound. There was a separate contained glass booth where Bas guessed someone would record vocals. Another side seemed to be a sitting area with comfortable chairs, a sofa, table, and a mini fridge, microwave, and coffee maker along with other supplies. To the right was an integrated sound booth with a variety of boards, recording equipment, and other things he didn't know. There were two places to sit and one seem to be occupied.

Instead of country rock, the speakers spilled Adam Lambert's sexy voice with one of Maroon 5's hits, *Moves Like Jagger*. A few steps from the sound booth, a slim fellow used some impressive moves as he belted out the vocals with Adam. It wasn't a half bad rendition, but Basil didn't know much about music other than he enjoyed listening to it and dancing at the clubs. Well, when he was able to dance all night at a club and pick up someone for a hot sweaty sex-filled night before returning to base.

Stepping inside, he closed the door softly and went to the closest post. He leaned his weight against it, taking his weight of his right leg and hip which was his bad side. He dug the heel of his hand into the taut muscle, massaging out the knots and tightness.

He skimmed his eyes down the slim fellow, dressed unlike any cowboy he ever met in his life. Skin-tight dark washed jeans looked like they were painted on those long legs and emphasized the gorgeous bubble butt. A narrow cut button-down shirt in pale pink hugged his upper body. Though slim, the fellow had a good pair of shoulders and arms with muscle to show he worked out. Snake-skin boots completed the stylish outfit that would be found in any popular city club instead of a horse ranch in the outskirts of Montana. As the man slowed down, Bas lifted his gaze to catch glimpses of a slender, almost feminine face with high cheekbones topped off with some type of glasses. He wore his coffee-dark hair shaved short around the sides and back, but left the top full and wavy, spiked and styled with gel.

This fella was one gorgeous package of a man.

When the song ended, Bas hung the cane from his forearm and clapped in appreciation of the impromptu performance.

The man must have jumped three feet straight up and spun to face him. Slender hands pressed against his chest as he tried to figure out how to breathe and talk again. "Holy Hannah!"

Bas lifted an eyebrow and smiled. "Sorry, I heard the music," he said, raising his voice as the next song started.

"What? Hold on, I can't hear you," the other man said and raced to the board. He hit something on a laptop and main board to turn off the music.

Grasping the cane once more, hating the use of it, Basil limped-stepped closer to the sound booth.

"What did you—" The other man spun around again as he talked and stopped short when Basil stood in front of him. "...say?" He ended with a softer tone. Behind the bronze metal framed glasses, his hazel-blue eyes widened slow and steady. Basil noticed the guy lined those beautiful eyes with sleek black boy eyeliner to go along with the slick lip balm covering his lips. He wondered what flavor those lips would taste like if kissed. A quick drop of his gaze to find the pale blue stick peeking out of a pocket. "Holy freaking Hannah!"

Basil blinked twice at the expression.

"You're...You're..." The man tried to push out, leaned to the side to see if anyone would rescue him, and stared again at Basil. "You're Basil. You're Sage's brother."

"Yup. How did you know?"

"Childhood meeting. Pictures." The man waved a hand between them. "What are you doing here? In Montana?"

"Charlie wrote to me and told me to get my ass home. I followed his orders," Basil said as he walked around the slender man to perch his tired ass on the closest stool. *Childhood meeting?* When did he ever meet this gorgeous boy during his childhood? Tilting his head, he stared at the other man, but unable to place the face. Is this why

Lorraine asked him if he recognized this man? Why couldn't he remember?

"Shit, you don't even remember me," the guy said as he stepped back and hooked his fingertips into the edges of the tight hip pockets. He stared down and scuffed his boots on the wooden planked floor.

"I'm sorry, but it completely dropped my mind. How do we know one another?"

"I was one of the mess of kids racing around with Sage. The ones you probably never paid attention too since you were busy with your friends, baseball, or practicing the rodeo."

Again, Basil tried to place the face. "I'm sorry."

"No problem. It's been a while. I changed and so did..." The guy waved a hand down Basil's tall frame. "You. Wow. A lot. You got...umm...tall."

Basil grinned and chuckled. Deciding to cut through the confusion, he held out his hand. "Basil Wallstatt."

Bouncing on his toes, impressive in both the tight jeans and boots, the guy stepped closer and took hold of Basil's hand. "Thomas. Thomas Bellamy."

"Bellamy?" Basil held on to the slender hand and tilted his head again. He knew the last name. "Are you Jacob's little brother?"

Thomas flushed and nodded. "Yes, I'm Jacob's little brother. All grown up."

Basil looked over Thomas again. "I would agree on that and I say you're on the rainbow spectrum."

Thomas laughed. "One way to put it, but yes, I am gay."

"Really..."

Thomas nodded again and tried to tug his hand back, but Basil didn't let go.

"How is your brother? What's he doing these days?"

Unable to pull away, Thomas stepped closer so he wouldn't stretch his arm. "Jacob is good. He's Deputy Sheriff and married to Virginia Harding."

"He married Ginnie. Good for him. Kids?"

"They have two boys and a third on the way. Ginnie is hoping for a girl, but they're keeping it a surprise until the birth."

"Congratulations to both of them. Do you talk to him?"

"Yes, he's not pissed at me."

"Unlike your parents."

"Conservative and religious as God Almighty. I never stood a chance." Thomas shrugged. "They left Montana and moved to Arizona when the bank foreclosed on the farm. Our other siblings scattered. Only Jacob and I remained behind."

"Why did you stay in Montana? Looking as cute as you do, you could have gone anywhere."

Another flush colored Thomas's face up to his ears. It was adorable as hell. "Umm. I hooked up with Sage and the band while I did the sound-work for the high school and drama club plays and concerts. Hold on. Wait a minute. Stop right there." He tugged his hand free and held them both up.

Acting all innocent to play with the cutie, Basil stayed quiet and let Thomas take his hand back. "What did I say?"

Thomas rolled one hand and held up a single finger. "Cute? Did you say I'm cute?"

"Is that bad?"

This time it was Thomas who gave Basil another long slow look from his dusty black combat boots to his disheveled hair. "No way are you gay, Sage would have said."

"Sage doesn't know everything."

"Are you? Gay?"

"Perhaps." Bas gave him a grin and wink.

"No freaking way."

Basil shrugged. Since leaving Montana and his father's hatred, he learned to accept his sexuality and lived it to the fullest. Sure, at the beginning until DADT was repealed, he had to be careful with his military career. Once things adjusted after the repeal, he was free to be himself amongst his friends. He kept the truth of his relationship with Larry between them throughout their careers. Even after Larry's death, he only offered his condolences as Larry's teammate and scout partner to his parents and nothing more.

"Oh, shit, oh, shit, oh shit..." Thomas bounced on his toes again, almost ready to burst out the seams.

"Is this a problem?"

"Don't know. Don't know. But oh shit... Sage is gonna flip," he said, his voice rising an octave with the last word.

Unable to get a read on Thomas, Basil pushed it aside. "How did you get about learning all this sound stuff? This thing is like what you see at concerts." He pointed his thumb at the sound booth next to him.

"Umm. Right. Sound tech. Umm." Thomas stopped bouncing and rubbed a hand over the back of his neck. Basil smiled at how a flustered rambling Thomas was even more adorable than the bouncing one. "Once we realized Midnight Twang wasn't disintegrating, I decided to follow my techie self and went to school. I got my training and finished an apprenticeship to become their journeyman sound technician. I never regretted coming back here. It's home. Sage made a place for me on the ranch."

"I don't see you riding around in those jeans."

Thomas rocked back on his heels and looked down. "Umm. I have more cowboy-like gear to wear, but mostly I stick around the main house and assist Lorraine." He dropped back on his heels and finally tugged his hand free. He covered his nervousness by tugging the lip balm stick from his pocket and slicked his lips.

Basil caught the light mint scent. *Would the taste fill a kiss?*

Capping the stick, Thomas pushed it back in the pocket and kept his fingers tucked inside the pocket. "How did we get to talking about me?"

"I'm good at deflecting questions," Basil said.

"That's not fair," Thomas said, turning to stare at him.

"Years of training and stealth required more action than talk." Basil stepped closer, backing Thomas against the board. "A little bit of planning in all things."

Thomas leaned back and lifted his gaze to meet Basil's stare. "What are you planning?"

"To steal a kiss and see what your lip balm tastes like."

Both of Thomas' eyebrows lifted.

With the decision to take a chance, Basil brushed his lips against the shiny mouth. Thomas' mouth was soft and supple. It did taste of mint. Everything about Thomas was addicting.

Too damn addicting.

Basil pulled back and stared down at him. Thomas closed his eyes, still leaning up toward him as if waiting for another kiss.

When it didn't come, Thomas opened his eyes with a few blinks and the becoming blush colored his cheeks.

Oh yes, this one will become an addiction.

At that moment, Stryker woofed for attention and raced over them, having made a sniff and check circuit around the place. He sat hard between them, his butt and tail wiggling.

Basil was grateful for the tension breaker between them.

Thomas laughed as he looked down at the adorable pup. He crouched down, another impressive feat in Basil's mind, to let Stryker sniff his hands. Once approved, he gave Stryker a full body scratch, pet, and ruffle which sent the dog in to full body adulations for more.

"You're his buddy for life by doing that," Basil said.

"He's the cutest little thing I've ever seen. What's his name? Is he yours?"

"More like I'm his hooman guardian, but yes, we belong together. His name is Stryker. He's a three-year-old black Labrador and Schnauzer mix with more of the Schnauzer in him based on his size and coloring. We met about six months ago at a shelter outside of Baltimore."

"Is that where you were?"

"For a while, yes, I was staying there."

Thomas looked up while continuing to give Stryker attention and belly rubs. "Sage is going to flip out when he sees you."

There was the 'flip' word again. Bas didn't know if he should freak out or not. "Flip out good? Flip out bad?"

"Don't know." Thomas turned his head. "Looks like you're going to find out though." He pointed his fingers toward the main doors.

Taking a deep breath, Basil turned on the stool.

His little brother, Sage, stood braced in the doorway. The last bit of the sunlight threw his face in shadows along with the ball cap pulled low on his forehead. Part of Basil wondered if that was the same cap their father gave Sage when they were younger, when things were still good between all of them. A taller man in a Stetson stood a little to the side of Sage, a protective hand curled around Sage's waist.

Silence filled the barn studio. Only the jingle of Stryker's tags cause a soft sound to break things, but it didn't help much.

Bracing himself between the table and closest column, Basil rose to his feet as he kept his gaze upon his little brother. He kept the cane hidden for the moment. He braced his body against the storm he knew would hit him hard.

"Hello, little brother," Bas said.

Those words seem to set Sage off. He raced over like a wild mustang and flailed his fists against Basil's chest. All kinds of accusations and curses left Sage as he tried to beat Basil to hell.

Ignoring the pain flowing through his body, Basil let his brother move through his anger, pain, and frustration. He damn well deserved every blow against his body. When Sage seem to lose the fight within him, Basil wrapped his arms around his brother. He cupped one hand around Sage's head, knocking the ball cap loose, pressing Sage against his chest. He curled his other arm around Sage's waist, bringing them closer. Tilting his head down, he tried to protect and comfort his brother with his body and voice.

Sage's upper body moved with short, erratic breathing until it broke into sobs, soul deep ones that ripped apart in pieces over the years. Sage embraced Basil, his hands grabbing hold of Basil's shirt, fisting them against his lower back. He pressed his face against Basil's chest, soaking the soft cotton shirt with his tears.

"Let it out. It's okay. I'm here now, little brother, I'm here. Let it out," Basil said, whispering similar words over and over as they rocked together through the storm of Sage's emotions. He didn't acknowledge the other two men who gathered around them, not even when Kaden crouched to pick up Sage's hat. He rubbed his hand in circles around Sage's back, impressed by how his little brother grew into a tall and powerful young man.

When the storm cleared, Sage stepped back, wiped his eyes with shirt sleeves. His eyes were puffy and tinged with red from the bout of crying. He lifted his gaze to take in Basil's height. "You got taller."

Basil laughed hard at the simple observation. "So did you, little brother."

"Yeah, well, that's what happens when you're gone for seventeen years. Bastard," Sage said without the earlier heat.

"Not all that happens," Basil said.

At that moment, his body turned against him. He felt his right hip and thigh begin to collapse on him.

"Fuck..." Basil muttered as he tried to brace himself against the pain. He tried to grab hold of the column, but missed.

Instead of falling to the ground, he stopped short when Thomas moved faster than him. Thomas appeared under his arm, wrapped his arms around his waist and supported Basil's weight to balance him. "Gotcha," he said.

"Thanks, appreciate it," Basil said, smiling down at Thomas, who adjusted his glasses which were knocked askew by the sudden movements. "Where's the cane?"

"Umm, I'm not sure. Something rattled my brain for a moment there."

Basil grinned, knowing the reason.

Thomas leaned away from Basil, still steadying him between his hands and looked around. "Kaden, can you grab the cane?"

Kaden circled them to pick it up and held it out Basil. "Here you go."

"Thanks, Kaden," Basil said as he gripped the handle and placed the cane firmly on the floor. He adjusted his weight and balance to use it for support. "Good to see you around here. You grew up fine too. I heard what you did for my brother and home. Thank you."

"Thanks, Basil. Didn't think we would see you again," Kaden said, holding out his hand. "As for what I did, well, I helped save my home too. It was only money."

Basil shook the younger man's hand. "Yeah, there were times I wasn't sure myself."

"How long have you been here?" Sage demanded, breaking the soft discussion.

"Less than a week."

"Did you visit Daddy?"

"I had a good long talk with him and straightened out a few things between us."

"Really?"

Basil nodded.

"About damn time. Why did no one tell us you were here?"

"I've been hiding in the house with Charlie and Lorraine. I wanted to wait for you and Kaden to return from your getaway, before seeing anyone else."

"Really? Why?"

"To see if I would still be welcomed back by you," Basil said, his tone softening.

Sage's eyes widened. He didn't give him an answer, but instead checked out Basil from head to feet, holding his gaze long on Basil's cane. "What the devil happened to you? What's with the cane?"

"Perhaps we should go over to the sitting area and you guys can sit and talk," Thomas suggested. "Sorry to butt in, but I don't think your brother can stay on his feet much longer."

"That would be better and you're correct. Some days I'm better, but it comes and goes. The nature of the injuries, I guess," Basil said. "Please, Sage?"

"Yeah, yeah. Sure." With some erratic movements that revealed his uncertainty and confusion, Sage let Kaden take him by the elbow and lead him across the studio to the comfortable seating area.

"Do you want my help?" Thomas asked, his tone soft.

"Please. As you said, I'm unsteady on my feet. Though I rested, the long hours of traveling didn't agree with me." Basil whistled to Stryker and pointed across the studio to tell the dog where to go.

Stryker rolled to his feet and bounded across. He went straight to Sage and Kaden, sniffing around their feet and lower legs to determine whether they were friend or foe. He wagged his tail to show his interest and exuberance for new smells and friends.

"Who is this?" Sage called out.

"Stryker, a rescue pup I adopted. He's friendly and loves attention," Basil said.

While Thomas helped Basil limp-step across the studio and into the closest armchair that would best support him, Stryker woofed and danced around Sage and Kaden, playing with them. Basil settled into the seat with a heavy sigh and moan. He would need to take one of the damn pain pills later or he would never get any sleep. Adjusting himself again, he set the cane aside and nodded to Thomas in thanks for the help.

"Do you guys want me to stick around? I can go and tell the others to leave you alone to talk," Thomas asked, looking between the brothers.

Basil watched Kaden take Sage's hand and whisper something. Sage quickly shook his head and covered their hands with his other hand to keep Kaden in place.

"You can stay, Thomas. Whatever we talk about I'm sure would get around the ranch in time. I'm not hiding any secrets. Not anymore," Basil said.

"Sage?" Thomas asked.

"I'm fine. Stay. Please," Sage said. "I want Kaden to stay too."

"Of course, Charlie told me you two got together. Congratulations to both of you," Basil said.

"You're not pissed?"

"Pissed?"

"Me being gay? Is that why you left? Cause you couldn't handle having a gay brother?" Sage demanded.

Laughing hard at the absurdity of the question, Basil pressed one hand to his lower ribs. He saw Sage's expression alter to one of annoyance and a flash of anger. He held up his other hand to ask for a moment to gather himself. "No. No. That wasn't why I left. Not at all. It had nothing to do with you," he said.

"Why the fuck did you stay away all this time? Why are you here now?"

"Damn, where do I start?" Basil trailed off as his thoughts wandered to the horrific fight with their father that altered the path of his life. He rubbed his hand up and down his thigh.

"The beginning is often a good point, not to be the annoying one for saying something obvious," Thomas said as he headed to the small fridge and pulled out four reusable water bottles.

"What's with the colors?" he asked while watching Thomas hand over two matching blue and green bottles to Sage and Kaden. He was given an orange topped one while Thomas held on to a black one.

"Different fellas like their drinks a certain way. At one-point things kept getting mixed up and we were going through a crap ton of cans and bottles. I'm the environmental nut of the group and it bothered the hell outta me. So I got online and ordered all of these to make everyone happy." Thomas pointed to Basil's bottle. "Orange is for guests and plain water."

"Fine by me. I'm restricted to water and herbal teas for a while," Basil said and muttered, "Damn, I miss coffee." With a shake of his head, he fiddled with the bottle in his hands.

Thomas perched on the arm of Basil's chair, as if offering a quiet show of support.

Swallowing once, Basil let his gaze drift down Thomas' slender back. The lower curve moved into the delicious bubble butt. He wondered how Thomas would feel underneath him. The sharp mint scent alerted to Thomas re-applying the lip balm. He lifted his gaze and watched Thomas meet it with a flicker of awareness.

Oh yes, definitely an addiction. This is a good one to have. It's full of pleasure and none of the darkness and pain.

With a grimace, Bas pulled himself away from the distracting thoughts. He didn't come home to seduce the younger brother of an old friend. There could be no more than the stolen kiss between them. Thomas and Sage obviously seemed close as well. He couldn't screw up with anything, not now when things were tentative and fragile.

"So...Are you going to tell me?" Sage asked, pushing his big brother.

"You know Dad and I argued throughout the week of my high school graduation. Right?" Basil asked, deciding to start there for simplistic reasons.

"Yeah, the whole damn ranch heard. What about it?"

"The weekend before graduation, he found me in the back stall of the barn."

"Sleeping on the job?"

"With another cowboy," Basil said.

Sage's jaw dropped. All color left his face.

"I was making out with Gage and there was no mistaking what we were doing."

"Gage? Gage Hawking?"

Basil nodded.

"He left the same week you did," Sage said.

Basil fiddled with the bottle. "He fled across the country and settled down in Atlanta, Georgia, last I heard. Dad didn't give either of us many options. He wasn't 'going to have no gawd-damned homo son owning and running his family's land. No way would he stand up to watch that happen.'" He altered his voice to sound more like their father's tone.

"Oh, shit, I knew things were different back then. I didn't know he went that deep," Sage said, leaning forward as he braced his elbows on his legs. He held his head between his hands, rubbing the light growth of whiskers against his fingers. Kaden moved his hand to rest it lightly on Sage's back, keeping them close.

"From what Charlie told me about when you came out to our parents, it was vastly different."

"You paid the price for my acceptance," Sage said, his voice tightened. "Oh, shit, damn, Bas..."

"It was one of things I talked about with Daddy. How it tore me apart to know I disappointed him so much and how his anger toward me twisted something inside me." Basil cleared his throat and pushed back the stinging in his eyes.

Thomas placed his hand on Basil's shoulder and squeezed.

Basil lifted his hand and touched Thomas' fingers, but let his hand drift back to his lap. He looked at his brother, watched Sage push his hair back from his face with fingers as if to use the pain. "Don't dwell on the anger, please. We can't change the past. It happened. We both survived through it."

Pressing his fingers to his mouth, Sage nodded.

"What about the Marines?" Kaden asked.

"After Dad blew up at me for several more days, threatening to send me to one of those Christian re-education camps that specialize in conversion of gay teens, I made the choice. Stick it out on the ranch and risk being sent to the camp or leave. Unlike Gage, I didn't have the resources to leave on my own. No car, no cash, and no other experience except for handling a place like this. I wouldn't have put it past Dad to call around several counties to black-ball me from any chance at a job. There was only one way. I went to the recruitment center three days before graduation, spoke about the different options, and went with the Marines. Dad taught me to use the long-range rifle and it gave me an advantage. After boot camp and gaining a certain level, I became a Scout Sniper."

"Sniper? I thought you were a Marines guard for one of the American embassy overseas," Sage asked.

"It was a convenient cover for some operations my platoon was sent in to handle."

"Good thing you followed Dad's teaching with the rifle, I couldn't do it. Not after one shot and I saw the life leave a doe's eyes," Sage said and shuddered from head to feet. "I swore then, I would only touch the damn thing to save the life of one of the horses or any of us. That's it."

"I took more than a doe's life, Sage. It wasn't all heroic."

Kaden gasped as if he figured something out and drew their attention. Sage sat straight up and pressed his hand to Kaden's chest.

"What? What happened?" Sage asked.

Kaden turned and stared straight at Basil.

Basil could see the realization and Kaden added up the time-line. He nodded and shrugged. "I was in Scout/Sniper school when the Towers fell."

"Oh shit, you were swept up in the shit storm after 9/11," Kaden said.

"For the majority of my military career, yes, I was in or around that mess."

"That's when Dad changed and I came out," Sage said. "He watched the Towers fall, the Pentagon go up in flames, and a plane crash due to the bravery of the passengers and he cried." Sage rubbed his hands together. "Our father cried and slammed his fists into the wall, over and over. He called out your name." He shook his head over and over, tears filling his eyes. "It's why he changed. He knew you would be in the thick of the fight and didn't want me to follow in your footsteps."

"At least something helped him see there was more to life than having a gay son," Basil said.

Rising from his seat, passing the bottle to Kaden, Sage rushed over to Basil's chair. He sat on the opposite arm from the quiet Thomas and wrapped his arms around Basil tight. He dropped his head until his forehead pressed against Basil's shoulder.

Reaching up, Basil embraced his little brother once again, accepting the love and comfort. "Ssh. I'm here. I made it through. So did you."

Pulling back, wiping his face with the backs of his hands, Sage stared at him. "I could have lost you. We would have never known until your fucking casket was delivered to us, you lunkhead." He punched Basil's shoulder without any power behind it. "Why didn't you write?"

"I did. After boot camp, I sent several letters home, mostly addressed to you. I explained my decision to leave and join the Marines, about my training, and other stuff. I sent them every other month for a year. Every single one came back— 'Refused / Return to Sender'. Every single one. After that I stopped writing," Basil said.

"Oh damn him, I never saw one letter. Never. You know I would never..."

"I know, little brother. He was upset and in a bad place."

"Did you know anything about what was happening around here?"

"Charlie wrote to me. Quite often. Lorraine sent me some awesome care packages. Her cookies were a huge hit when you're stuck out in the middle of the desert."

"Why didn't you respond to the certified letters by the bank? I had to deal with a lot of shit from the bank and came close to losing our home because I couldn't do things like you or Dad," Sage said as he slid off the arm and crouched next to his brother.

"Five years ago, I was in a major accident." Basil swallowed hard. "It was fatal for members of my team." He swallowed again to push back the lump in his throat. When he tried to play with the seam of his pants again to distract himself from the pain, he watched Sage cover his hand and hold them together. "The helicopter I was traveling back from a mission along with my spotter, other members of the platoon, and the Black Hawk crew went down. I didn't properly do my job on the ground. I missed a sniper in the darkness. He didn't miss his shot to the engines." He closed his eyes and held his mouth in a tight thin line.

As a soft hand rubbed circles on his back and warmth against his side, Basil opened his eyes and found Thomas leaning closer. Even Kaden shifted to the end of the sofa to be closer to them.

"You survived," Sage said.

"I was the only survivor. Two others survived the crash, but not their injuries. Out of eleven passengers in the Black Hawk, six Marines are dead and four crewmembers are dead from either the crash or injuries caused by it. I'm the only survivor, but..."

"You're still working on healing, more than just your body," Thomas said, his voice soft.

Basil glanced over to Thomas. "Every damn day."

"You lost someone close in that crash. It was someone closer than the rest of your brothers on the team. Didn't you?" Thomas' gaze quiet but knowing behind the thin frames.

"My spotter. We were matched during school and stayed a team throughout our careers. We were closer than brothers because we had to read each other when on a mission. He picked out my targets with me, giving me information, and I took the shots. We were thick as thieves, you could say." Basil licked his lower lip.

"You guys started something deeper."

"First, we fooled around when off base. Then as the fighting became worse, it turned into more. We swore it would never interfere with our jobs and it didn't. Until the crash when I screamed his name, reaching for him, but watched him whisper my name and slip away." Basil clenched his free hand and shook his head.

"It's okay. You don't need to say anything more," Thomas said as he tried to get Basil to lean against him.

Giving in to the gentle pressure, Basil rested against Thomas' side and breathed past the lump in his chest. What was it about this younger man that drew him and made him feel more grounded than ever before? At the same time, he felt Sage squeeze their hands together.

"A little broken. A little battered. A little weary. But you're home. Home with us," Sage said as he rose to his feet. "You're not leaving anytime soon. Got it?"

"No plans to leave. Charlie filled me in on everything else happening around here over the last couple of nights. He told me about Mama's health."

Dipping his head down, Sage squeezed their hands again. "Yeah. It isn't the best situation."

"Can we see her?"

"I'll ask Doc Evan tonight. Until the cancer got bad, I couldn't get close. Mama lived in a time where she was a newlywed with Dad in the little cabin. Before she had kids. Even introducing us as neighbors or visitors didn't work. It agitated her," Sage said.

"What about now?"

"Doc Evan said the medication has her drifting in and out. There's no other way to keep her comfortable. Fucking cancer," Sage said. "I thought the Alzheimer's was bad, stealing her memories and sense of self, the cancer is worse. It's eating her from the inside out and taking its sweet old time."

Rising from his chair, pushing up against the chairs' arms and Thomas' support, Basil tugged Sage in for another embrace. "Together, little brother. We'll handle everything together. From here on out, I promise I'm not going anywhere."

For a bunch of cowboys, there was a lot of hugging and crying around here, but Basil wouldn't have it any other way.

"Holding you to it, brother."

After all the drama in the barn, Thomas didn't want to leave them to help Lorraine, but he wouldn't slack on his job. At least he finally figured out the mystery of the unknown guest he kept seeing every morning. *Then there was that sneaky kiss. What the devil did he mean by doing that? Holy Hannah, it knocked me off my feet.* Bouncing into the kitchen, Thomas slid into the rainbow apron and washed his hands.

"Where have you been? I was going to send out someone to look for you," Lorraine asked as she slid over a pile of vegetables, board and salad bowl. "Set up the salad."

"Sorry, lost track of time in the barn. Then a certain unknown fella entered. Holy Hannah, the guy is Sage's brother! Why didn't you tell me Basil Wallstatt was home?" Thomas shoved hands on his hips, tapped his boot, and stared at Lorraine.

"It wasn't my position. He didn't want anyone but Charlie and I to know of his arrival until he spoke with Sage. There's a lot on his plate that he's dealing with, honey. He's worrying about his Mama, his health, and now his relationship with Sage. Did he speak with Sage?"

"Oh boy, did he ever speak with Sage. Kaden too."

"What? When did they find one another?"

"Sage and Kaden entered the barn after I was talking with Basil."

"Talking or flirting?"

Thomas felt the heat of a flush crept across his face. To wait until he calmed down, he dug the lip balm stick from his pocket and slicked his lips again. He couldn't believe it when he caught Basil watching him apply the lip balm with heat building in those bright blue eyes.

"Hmm. Just what I thought. You're still hot about him after all this time."

"Yes, well..." Thomas shrugged. "Come on, he was this big hero of my childhood. He hung out with Jake and all that rodeo stuff, while letting us little kids tag along. I couldn't help it. I knew then I was different, checking out the boys in magazines and not the girls. I didn't want to get rough and dirty with the boys, but forced myself to fit in."

"How was it seeing him all over again?"

To his utter embarrassment, Thomas muttered, "He didn't recognize me."

"That's what I thought."

"What?"

"He checked you out a couple of days ago when he stopped by the kitchen for a to-go breakfast."

"He had no clue who I was?"

"Sorry, baby. Like I said, that man has a lot on his mind."

"Okay, I can handle that. Still, it's a complete utter embarrassment on my end. My hero. My crush. Vamoose—I'm nothing to him. Why did it have to be me?" Thomas stomped to the closest wall and banged his forehead twice to vent his frustration.

Lorraine chuckled at his diva antics. "Oh, baby, it was over seventeen years and you grew up. You don't resemble the little awkward boy from back then."

"Do you think I'm too femme for someone like him?"

"I don't know, baby, but as I said he was checking you out."

"Did he say anything?"

"Only that you were adorable."

"Adorable? That's it."

"And his body may be battered, but it wasn't dead. There could be a flicker of hope, but no one can know what another heart desires."

Thomas returned to the counter. "I'm not gonna give up hoping. I can work with adorable and a flicker. I don't give up easily. Nope.

Not this blasted peacock." With his determination firmly in place, he stomped a boot to solidify it. "I can work with one measly kiss."

"Kiss? What kiss?"

"Oh, um, nothing much since it was only a tease. Honest," Thomas said.

"That's an interesting twist. I didn't know he still knew how to play and tease."

"It seems he can play when he wants."

"Perhaps when he's with you, he feels free. Basil is home and safe. He's able to safely come out to us and be himself. Anything could happen, baby," Lorraine said.

Grumbling about he would dance and flash his 'tail' to attract his mate, Thomas made plans in his head while he washed, spun, and tore apart the lettuce leaves. He worked his way through the rest of the vegetables, built the salad, and finished it with homemade vinaigrette dressing and croutons. Tossing everything together, he carried the bowl to the side table and set it in place.

When the four roasted pork loins came out of the oven and rested, Thomas sliced through all of them. He laid them out on a platter with the bowl of mushroom-shallot gravy next to it. He tossed the green beans with their bacon and sliced almond dressing and poured them into another serving dish. Roasted sweet potatoes and a rice pilaf finished off the side dishes. While he mixed up two pitchers of sweet iced tea and fresh lemonade, Lorraine rang the bells to call everyone to the evening meal.

With dinner over and most of the cowboys headed out to either the bunkhouses or into town, Thomas rose to begin cleaning up the mess. It wasn't the favorite part of his job, but he did it. It was nice when others jumped in to help. This time, Simon, who played the mandolin, slide guitar and banjo for the band, was the first to get up and help. He nudged Andrew, the band's piano player, to also help them. Between the three of them, they made quick work of clearing the dishes from the table and buffet. Thomas emptied the dishwasher from an earlier round and loaded it back up while Simon scraped everything clean.

At the same time, they listened in to the conversation happing at the dining table. Thanks to the remodel, they could watch everything happening around the table while cleaning. The old kitchen had been cut off from everything and it sucked when it came to cleaning.

"So... What do you think about having him home? Think it's going to change anything?" Simon asked in a lower tone.

"Don't know. He looks a little wobbly. What kind of accident was he in? Doesn't look like he's able to get on a horse and help much," Andrew said as he packed up the leftovers.

"Hey! Watch what you're saying," Thomas snapped as he stopped his work and held Andrew in his gaze. "That man out there was injured protecting our country after 9/11. A little respect is due to him, Andrew. He went through hell to get to where he is. It took a lot for him to come home and sit out there with his family."

"Shit, I'm sorry, Thomas," Andrew said as he held his hands up and backed away from Thomas.

Both of his friends were a little shocked at how Thomas snapped. It was out of character for him, but this was Basil. The Basil he knew since he was a boy. No one would talk bad about him, not in front of Thomas.

"I'm just saying to make a point. Get the facts before you say something like that," Thomas said.

"I know. Sorry. No filter."

"It doesn't excuse the rudeness. As for not being able to ride, who cares. There's other jobs around here. I don't ride and I'm still productive."

Simon moved his head between them like watching a tennis match. "Sheesh. Knock it off, you two." He gathered the nearest towel and tossed it at Andrew's face. "Go wipe down the buffet."

Andrew caught the towel before it slapped him and walked away.

"Okay. Spill. What got into you?" Simon asked.

"Nothing. Basil was and is a Marine. It's a helluva lot more to do that than anything here," Thomas said.

As he listened, Simon straightened and stopped mid-scoop to drop the remaining leftovers in a container. He pointed the utensil at Thomas and wiggled it. "You like him."

Thomas glanced toward the table and back to Simon. "Ssh!" he hissed and kept his attention on the sink to stop the conversation.

"Crap. You *like* him. I mean *like him like* him. A lot." Simon chuckled and Thomas knew there would be hell to pay when the others learn. "Is this the one you were talking about when Josh asked if you had someone? You meant Basil Wallstatt? Holy crap!"

"I was a damn kid and he was best friends with my brother. They were a dominant force in my life, same as Sage. We looked up to them."

"But you like him," Simon said, pushing a finger into Thomas's shoulder.

"Shut up." Flushed at how Simon remembered that damn conversation, Thomas cleared his throat and turned away. He left Simon to finish the loading and returned to the table, reaching out to gather the left-over items like napkins, utensils, and other things. He caught everyone in mid-conversation and listened in like a shameless hussy.

"You're more than welcomed to find me anytime, Basil. I would be happy to check over your injuries for healing and offer some additional stretching and therapy," Doctor Evan Sampson said. Doc Evan was the latest addition to the ranch after falling hard in love with the band's fiddler, Joshua Holmwood.

Still recovering from an accident that broke a wrist and surgery to repair other injuries, Josh couldn't pick up his fiddle for another three months to even practice. He wouldn't be back to full strength and capacity for playing in an all-night concert for the rest of the year. It bothered everyone since the rumors of a contract grew louder, but no one would think of replacing Josh. He had such a unique sound and talent on the fiddle, which caused Sage to snatch him up for the band. No one could match him so they all chose to wait for Josh to heal.

For now, Josh leaned against Doc Evan's shoulder. His elbows were wrapped with Ace bandages for the evening along with the one wrist that had been broken by a wild mustang.

"I appreciate that, Doc. My doctors were worried I wouldn't get the care I need up here," Basil said.

Thomas froze when Basil lifted and fixed his intense blue gaze upon him. He grinned and returned to work.

"You mentioned you had third-degree burns. May I ask where?"

"Lower back and right hip were the worse. I had multiple grafts to both areas to fill in the lost tissue and muscle," Basil said. "Don't want to drop pants here since it isn't a pleasant thing to look at after a wonderful meal."

"I do have a no-flash policy at the table," Lorraine said with a sharp tone, which caused everyone to laugh.

"Yes, ma'am." Basil glanced back to Thomas, who had flushed at the thought of looking at such a fine ass.

Thomas didn't care how many scars covered Basil's body. All that mattered was that body, that man, was home.

Clearing his throat, Basil returned his attention to the doctor. "The rest were a mixture of first and second degree along with some busted bones. I was near one of the doors of the chopper and got tossed out at one point while others never made it out."

"That's a lot of trauma to heal," Doc Evan said.

"Still working on bits and pieces of it. One of them would be to have a decent night's sleep," Basil admitted and looked at his brother. "Well, little brother, I assume you and Kaden took over the master suite."

"Even renovated it. All ours," Sage said.

"Not moving," Kaden added.

Basil chuckled. "Not interested in doing stairs more than I need for therapy sessions. Thank you. What suites are left downstairs?"

"Where did you sleep?" Sage asked.

"I took one of the small rooms in the back. The ones for the late-night cowboys or other staff," Basil said. "I didn't want to make myself at home until we spoke."

"Bas, come on, I wouldn't kick you out," Sage said.

"You had every right, as I told you in the barn," Basil said.

"The suite behind the office and across from mine is open," Thomas said. "It has a king-size bed for you. The bathroom has both a large soaker tub and a shower stall."

"When did we get that one?"

"The remodel," Sage said. "Except for the entrance, living room, and office, everything else shifted positions around the first floor as it was extended."

"Thought things were in odd places when I first arrived. Kept turning into the damn hall closet," Basil said.

Everyone laughed at the confusion.

"Happened to everyone after construction finished," Sage said.

"Oh, good, I wasn't the only confused idiot." Basil flashed them a quick smile. "That suite can be mine."

"Whatever you want, brother," Sage said.

"I'll take it. Tomorrow we can start figuring out how I can be useful around this place. I can't stand to sit around without doing anything. No matter how much pain I'm in, I have to keep busy."

"Do you like paperwork?" Kaden asked in a hopeful tone while Sage and Charlie chuckled.

"I think I can learn to like it. Charlie and I went through some of it the night I arrived."

"Yes!" Kaden shot up both hands in a triumphant pose. He and Sage did a crazy chair dance and chanted a silly 'no more paperwork' song.

Closest to them, Thomas tugged the towel from his waist and snapped it against both of their shoulders.

"Ow!"

"Hey!"

"Don't bother with these chuckleheads," Thomas said. "Lemme finish up, and I'll show you to the suite."

"Appreciate it," Basil said.

"Time for you to do your exercises," Doc Evan told Josh, who grimaced. "If you want to play again, you'll follow my orders."

"And what happens if I'm a good boy?" Josh asked with a hopeful look on his face.

"We'll see..." Evan said as he rose with Josh and headed to the archway.

"Yeah, we all know what his reward will be!" Kaden called out in an obnoxious tone.

"Yeah, we all heard how much he loves his rewards," Sage added with a playful whistle.

Josh leaned around the corner and stuck out his tongue. "Not like you two don't do the same. Sound flows both ways, boys," he taunted back.

"Why you..." Sage rushed out with Kaden next to him. Soon they were hot on the other couple's tails, chasing them up the stairs.

"Is it always like this?" Basil asked as the pounding and stomping on feet continued overhead.

"Whenever they feel frisky, yup, and with them it means every night." Thomas returned to the kitchen.

"This is where we old folks say good night and sleep well," Charlie said as he stood and helped Lorraine out of her chair.

"Night!" Thomas called out from the kitchen. It was followed by calls from Simon and Andrew.

Basil's tone was softer and lower to the older couple.

Within a few more minutes, the dishwasher running, and the kitchen ready for the morning meal, Thomas waved good night to Simon and Andrew. He turned off lights and found Basil sitting in the armchair in the living room, a cup of water in one hand. A glance down revealed a quiet Stryker curled up by his feet.

"Hey there," Thomas said.

Basil turned and smiled. "Are you all done in there?"

"Yes, but it starts all over again tomorrow. Would you like me to take Stryker out for his evening walk? I don't mind at all," Thomas said.

Stryker lifted his head from his paws with a soft whine.

"That would be great. I need to take some medication and I'll pack up what little I pulled out in the other room. Meet you back here?"

"Sure. Ten minutes?"

"Not even. Appreciate it," Basil said as he set the glass down, pushed himself to his feet, and picked the glass back up. "Go on with Thomas, boy."

With a soft bark, Stryker got to his paws and trotted to Thomas. After a crouch to give the pup a scratch, Thomas took him outside and let him race around the back of the main house. He kept his gaze upon the black and white pup while he sniffed to find the perfect spot to do his nightly business. As he waited, Thomas leaned against the railing, lifting his face to meet the soft breeze, and let out a sigh.

Once his business was done, Stryker raced back to the porch and Thomas without a word from him.

"You're such a good boy. Such a smart pup," Thomas said, giving the pup more attention and loving.

They returned inside to find Basil waiting, a large canvas sea bag leaning against his leg and a backpack resting on the back of the chair.

"Want me to hold the backpack?" Thomas asked as he walked over.

"Sure," Basil said.

As he stepped closer to Basil, Thomas lifted his gaze to meet Basil's stare. He glanced down fast and reached for the backpack.

"Why are you shy with me? I'm the one who stole the kiss, not you," Basil said, his tone soft in the shadowed room. He brushed his fingers along Thomas' cheek.

Thomas flushed at the mention of it, but knew he wanted more of those kisses. Why did he feel so odd to be alone with Basil? They were alone in the studio, but this time... This time it felt different. He swallowed. "Been a while since I saw you and... It's nothing."

"Tell me."

"Childhood crush," he whispered the words.

It took a few minutes, but a soft whoosh of understanding left Basil. "Me?"

Thomas nodded.

"I'm flattered. I'm not the same boy I was then."

"Neither am I," Thomas said and returned his gaze back to Basil. This time he didn't flinch or drift away.

"So..." Basil let the word linger between them. "We see where this goes."

"This?"

"Attraction. I can tell you feel it too." He leaned closer to whisper the word again in Thomas' ear. "It's why I stole a kiss."

Thomas shifted at the warm air against the sensitive skin. He tilted his head and found their faces so close together. Lips almost meeting. This time he took the initiative and lifted up on his toes. Their lips met.

The kiss was soft, hesitant, and gentle as they learned everything about one another. It wasn't harsh or greedy. Their lips brushed against one another, pressing and opening, and sliding away until another motion brought them back together.

One of them moaned.

Thomas didn't know who, but he dropped back on his heels. He met Basil's stare as he reached up to touch Basil's face with his fingers. "Now we're even on the stealing part."

"Then everything will be mutual after this." Basil flashed his grin in the darkness. "Can you show me to my room?"

"Sure." Flustered, Thomas pressed his fingers to his swollen lips. *Oh yes, there would be many more kisses.* He hiked the backpack higher on his shoulder and led them down the suite. Even in the darkness, he swore he felt Basil's gaze watching his ass move. It was a damn good feeling.

Chapter Seven

After helping Basil settle in the room, leaving him to unpack and make it his place, Thomas went to his suite and closed the door. He went through his usual nighttime routine by stripping off the day's outfit, pulling on a super soft cotton robe, and moving to the bathroom. He sat on the stool in front of the counter and wiped off the eyeliner. With his face clean, he dropped the robe and showered. A quick dry to whisk away the droplets, he slid back into the robe, tying it in place and concentrated on drying his hair. Once he applied a little conditioner and frizz stuff, he let the rest air dry. After he finished the rest of his prep, he finished in the bathroom.

As he returned to the bedroom, he scooped up the old clothes and brought them to the hamper. He stood in the walk-in closet, studying the hangers to choose tomorrow's outfit. Since he always took forever to make up his mind, he learned to select the outfit the night before and handle the accessories and finishing touches in the morning.

Unlike the other gay males on the ranch, Thomas loved playing around with clothes. It didn't matter whether he was on the ranch or at a concert in the dark sound pit. Once he made the decision to no longer hide his true nature, he let his colors fly. It was another reason for the peacock title.

Making a choice, he selected sleek khaki pants as a change from the jeans, a white Henley shirt, and an aqua blue V-neck sweater. The super-fine cotton sweater was so lightweight he could see the underlying shirt. He finished the outfit with a dark leather belt and boots. Once he hung the ensemble from the door, he brushed out the imaginary flecks of fuzz and wrinkles.

Finished, he went to the dresser he shoved inside the closest and tugged out a pair of sleep pants. He stepped into them and tied the drawstring at his waist. As he left, he clicked off the lights. By the guidance of moonlight, he tugged back the covers, removed the robe, and slid under the crisp cotton sheets.

While he let his mind wind down after the crazy day, he played around on his tablet, pulling up the latest Angry Birds game to fling some birds at laughing pigs. It was mindless entertainment as he moved through the levels until sleep tugged at him. Saving and closing the game, he checked all of the alarms and slid into sleep.

A blood-curdling scream jolted Thomas straight out of his sleep. He jumped so hard, he literally fell out of the bed, tangled in the sheets. After he rubbed his sore ass and neck, he tried to untangle himself.

Another cry called out.

Barking followed.

"Holy Hannah!" Thomas realized what was happening. "Basil..."

He scrambled to get out of the sheets, raced around the bed toward the door. He yelped when his foot hit a corner of something, but he ignored the pain. With a yank on his door and a push on the closed door across from him, he stumbled into the other dark room.

Something soft and furry rubbed against his legs. Whines told him it was Stryker.

"Ssh. Easy, boy. I'm here," Thomas said as he hit the light.

With a blink to adjust to the sudden brightness, he found Basil stretched out on his back across the king mattress. A sheet tangled around his lower body. His upper chest was slick with sweat. His hands flailed and stretched out for something or someone in his dream.

Another horrible, pain-filled cry filled the room.

"Lawrence! No! Stay with me," Basil cried out.

Unable to stay put and let the damn nightmare hurt Basil any longer, Thomas went to the bed. He kept away from Basil's fists, not wanting to get punched by accident. He had to get Basil's attention somehow and pull him out of the dream.

"Holy crap! Be careful, Thomas, he has no idea where he is," someone called out.

A rumpled Doc Evan and Josh stood in the doorway. Evan stepped closer, holding his hands out to stop Thomas.

"What should I do? We can't leave him in this nightmare."

"Lawrence! Stay with me!" Basil shouted on the tail end of another pain-filled cry. He sat straight up, his eyes opened wide, and he let out another blood-curdling scream.

Thomas jumped in the air, scared out of his skin. He pressed both hands to his chest.

"This isn't a nightmare. This is a night terror and they're a little more difficult," Evan said in his calm doctor's tone.

"What the fuck is happening?" Kaden asked as he and Sage appeared behind Josh, who held out his arms to hold them back.

Sage lifted on his toes to look over and at his brother. "Basil! What's happening?"

"Sage, Kaden, please. We can handle this. Keep calm and in the hallway," Evan said. He kept his attention on Basil, who fell back and thrashed again.

"He's in pain," Sage said.

"He's trapped in a night terror. We'll get him out."

Thomas looked from Basil to the doctor. "What can we do?"

"He won't respond to our voices and will be hard to wake up, but it is possible. Once he does, he's going to be very lost and confused by what happened. It could take a long time to comfort and calm him down. Can you handle this?"

"Yes. Yes. I'll do anything to help him."

"Here's the bad part," Evan said.

"What?"

"We have to let it run its course. He'll wake up on his own as part of the cycle. Now that I know he suffers from them, I'll be able to help treat him for the nights to come."

"We have to let him go through this alone," Thomas said, waving a hand at the distressed Basil, calling and moaning for Lawrence.

"Other than prevent him from falling out of bed or doing harm to himself, especially with his previous injuries, it's all we can do. I'm sorry. There isn't always a quick fix."

Thomas shoved the fingers of both hands through his hair.

"Sage, Kaden, Josh, it's best for you guys to go back upstairs. I know this is scary for everyone. I don't want him to wake up surrounded. It could make the situation worse. Please," Evan said.

"He's my brother—" Sage tried to protest.

"Let Thomas help him. Basil will be embarrassed if he finds you holding him. He's a Marine. He doesn't want to appear weak. There's a connection between him and Thomas. It'll help," Evan said, his explanation simple and calm.

Sage looked at the doctor and over to Thomas. "Take care of him."

"With my life, I promise I'll help him," Thomas said.

Sage let Kaden lead him back upstairs, arm wrapped around him.

Josh leaned into Evan, whispering something to his lover, and pressed their lips together in a soft kiss. As he pulled back, he waved to Thomas and left them. Along the way, he managed to coax Stryker to follow him.

Thomas returned his attention to the bed while Evan entered the room, looked around, and walked over with a wastebasket.

"What's that for?" Thomas asked.

"In case he has nausea upon wakening. When he does, I want you to keep your tone soft and help him focus on the present and you. Help him control his breathing. It'll help steady him and bring him out of the terror completely, but it's a slow process."

"How will we know when it's done?"

As he finished the questions, it appeared a jolt of electricity went through Basil. He shot straight up in bed, looking around, as his breath sawed in and out of his lungs. "What— Who—No— Where—" He ran his hands over his body and looked under the covers. "Flames... No—" He stopped as he made a horrible retching sound.

Thomas sat on the edge of the bed and shoved the wastebasket under Basil in time. He turned away as Basil emptied his stomach. When he finished, Thomas dropped it to the floor.

"Basil, Basil, can you hear me? I need you to look at me, Basil," he said as he kept his voice low. He hated seeing the wild, confused look upon Basil's face. The wild-eyed gaze met and flirted with his steady stare. "There you are. Concentrate on your breathing. Slow it down. Pull it all the way in. Blow it all out." Thomas slid his fingers around one of Basil's hands, spread the clenched fingers out and pressed them to his chest. "Follow along with me. Listen to my breathing."

Throughout the next hour, Thomas worked steadily to console and comfort Basil. As the time lapsed, he could see Basil returning to awareness. He didn't listen as Evan cleaned up the mess and left them alone. When he left the bedroom, Evan closed the door to give them privacy.

Basil tilted his head. He blinked and focused. "Thomas..." he whispered, his voice hoarse from the screams.

"Yes, it's me. You're back with me." Thomas curled his palm around Basil's whiskered cheek.

Basil licked his lower lip. "What—"

"According to the doc, you suffered a night terror."

As he closed his eyes, Basil let out a soft curse. "Thought those left me alone. Had them when I arrived at rehab facility and stressed about the recovery."

"Perhaps the stress of coming back home triggered them again."

"Did I hurt anyone?"

"No. No. Evan kept us back from you. He knew what to do. You were calling for Lawrence."

"My partner, he died in the accident. I watched him die." With a licking of his lower lip again, Basil grimaced. "Damn. My mouth tastes like something died in it."

"Hold on. I'll be right back." Thomas left the bed and went to the bathroom. He filled a glass with water, found a second glass and a small bottle of mouthwash. He returned and set the items on the nightstand. "Here. Rinse and spit in here a couple of times. Follow up with the mouthwash."

"I threw up. Didn't I?"

"We caught it in the wastebasket. No mess to clean up."

With a nod, Basil concentrated on swishing and cleaning his mouth. When he finished the mouthwash, he wiped the back of his hand against his mouth. "Thanks."

"Welcome. Be right back." Thomas returned to the bathroom, rinsed everything, and found a washcloth. He got it wet and walked back. He tugged on the sheet to let it fall down around Basil's hips. He wiped away most of the gathered, drying sweat from his chest and belly.

"I'm a stitched-up freak to look at," Basil said. "I can do it."

"No. Let me," Thomas said in a stubborn tone. "As for being a freak, I don't agree with it. You're an honorable Marine who paid a high price to be alive. Your body reveals what you went through. I'm not turned off by it."

Basil covered Thomas' hand with his fingers to stop the movement. "Thank you for being here."

Thomas lifted his gaze to meet Basil's stare. "You're welcome."

"Damn, sorry. Stryker. Is he—"

"A little concerned and frightened, but Josh managed to coax him out. I'm sure Evan and Josh are cuddling the pup on their bed. He's in good hands."

"Good. Good. Didn't mean to frighten the poor pup."

"Give him lots of hugs and treats tomorrow and he'll be okay. He has a sweet forgiving nature to him." Thomas flipped the cloth to a new side and wiped it around Basil's back. He managed to get as far as his tailbone, but no further. The cloth tugged and flowed different as he discovered the deep scars, puckered skin, and glossy lines spreading across Basil's back and closest hip. He felt the same thing ran down Basil's thighs.

"Personal question, but…" Thomas played with the edge of the sheet between his fingers. "What about…"

"I'm still whole and in working order. Somehow the flames didn't reach there because I curled into a fetal position," Basil said with a wry grin.

"That's a checkmark in the positive column."

Basil let out a harsh chuckle. "Randall said something similar."

"So I wasn't the first to ask."

Basil shook his head. "About done?"

"I think I got most of it. See if you can get comfortable. We can change the sheets if you want," Thomas said as he walked to the bathroom. He rinsed out the cloth and left it on the counter. As he left, he flicked off the light.

The mattress squeaked and moved as Basil adjusted his body, the pillows and sheets. "No, the sheets are fine."

Thomas stood at the side of the bed. "How are you doing?"

"Yeah. Umm…" Basil glanced up under long lashes. "Stay with me?"

"Will it help?"

"I don't want to be alone."

"Sure. Let me turn off the rest of the lights and I'll return. What side?"

"The left will be more comfortable."

"Works for me," Thomas said and walked away. He pulled in a deep breath and released it at the thought of sleeping curled up against Basil's big body. He turned off the lights in his room, the hallway, and back in Basil's room. Thanks to memory, he found his way to the far side and slid under the sheet.

Shifting across the vast expanse until his leg touched one of Basil's legs, Thomas searched for a pillow and curled on his side.

"Could you? Like this," Basil said as he tugged and maneuvered Thomas close until he stretched out across Basil's side, using him as a full-length body pillow.

Thomas settled his cheek on Basil's chest. He lifted his head to look at Basil. "Are you okay?"

"Could you give me a kiss?"

"Kiss?"

"To steady my nerves?"

"Is that all?"

"To remind me I'm still here," Basil admitted.

Thomas placed his hand lightly on Basil's chest and shifted forward. He placed his lips against Basil's mouth. He let the kiss linger. He gave a soft moan when Basil slid his fingers into Thomas' hair to hold him closer. He opened his eyes and met Basil's gaze.

Bail leaned his head back and a smile curled his mouth. "Thank you. Curl closer to me, please."

With a nod, Thomas rested his cheek on Basil's shoulder. He rested his hand on his waist, just above the boxer's waistband and sheet. He pulled up one of his legs and placed it between Basil's legs. "Do you want me like this?"

"Perfect," Basil said.

Thomas felt Basil place a kiss in his hair and he closed his eyes at the sensation. Right where he wanted to be and could do nothing more except for sleep.

"Night," Basil murmured.

"Night, Basil. Sleep well," Thomas said as he couldn't stop himself. He pressed his lips to Basil's chest. While he breathed in the rich masculine scent tinged with a bit of citrus from some type of soap, he used it to calm his mind as he listened to the steady beating of Basil's heart. He let it lull him into sleep.

Chapter Eight

A week had passed since the disturbing night terror, Basil didn't want a repeat after one of those nights. He asked Doc Evan to speak with his therapist back in Baltimore, Daryl, to discuss the issues and possible causes. Both of them told him he could still be suppressing the memories and emotions from the helicopter accident and loss of his partner. Those emotions would rise when he was vulnerable at night and express themselves as the night terrors.

Daryl told Basil to call him anytime and they could have sessions over the phone or via FaceTime. As of this morning, Basil hadn't made either the call or appointment. How could he talk to Daryl about losing Larry when he couldn't even go near the memories on his own? He even skipped over most of those thoughts in his journal, something no one else read, but he didn't dare write them down. If he wrote them down, he feared everything would be true. He couldn't handle all of the truth. Not yet. He knew that part damn well.

It was a precarious battle.

Instead of dwelling on the memories, Basil enjoyed the good moments of the past week. One of them was how he became closer with Thomas. The sweet man had centered him after the terror, listened to him babble on as he found his way out of the disorientation, and cleaned him up— even the puke and ragged skin— without a wince of fear or pity. The kiss shared between them settled the rest of his internal pain from the night terror, from seeing Larry die repeatedly in his dreams. He looked at Thomas deeper than the flashy clothes and almost diva attitude, he was filled with a sweet charm underneath.

When he left, Thomas was a couple of years older than Sage, so yeah, he wasn't looking back then at the younger crowd. His heart had been set on a fellow teen cowboy, Gage. Of course that blew up on him when his daddy found them.

All these years later, Thomas blossomed into a happy, proud gay man who was sure of himself, his style and that zingy attitude he brought with him. The whole package melted into the walls around Basil's heart and they cracked apart. When he wasn't working in the office, he lingered in the kitchen, talking to him and Lorraine, helping when he could so he wouldn't be in the way. It became a thing for them, but often Lorraine left them alone. Other times, he made his way to the music barn, sat near Thomas and listened to his brother and the band work through song arrangements and practice. Josh often stayed with them too, still not allowed to lift his violin, but Thomas said he no longer acted like a whiny toddler. Basil could only laugh at the thought.

With those happier times whirling around in his head, Basil stood outside with his brother and family as they waited for their sister, Rosemary, and her family to arrive from Kalispell.

Snazzy and sexy in his crisp pale green shirt and dark wash jeans, Thomas walked over to stand next to him.

"Barbecue ready to go?" he asked Thomas.

"Smoker's been going since dawn and under Simon's careful watch. He's the barbecue guru of the group when he's not playing a mean slide guitar," Thomas said.

Basil chuckled. "I look forward to tasting his offerings. What's in the smoker?"

"Brisket and ribs with a side of pork butt. Gotta have some butt in there."

Basil laughed louder until his belly hurt. His brother and Kaden looked at him strange.

"What did you say to him?" Sage asked Thomas.

"Gotta have some butt in the smoker," Thomas said with a cheeky grin.

Sage joined Basil in the laughter. Others joined in the merriment.

When he calmed down, wheezing to breathe, Basil wrapped one arm around Thomas' shoulders and tugged him close for a hug. He lowered his head and took a moment to breathe in the delicious scent of the man. "What do you use in the shower that smells so damn good?" he whispered so only Thomas could hear.

"It's called..." Thomas paused and pushed out his hand in front of him as he said in a dramatic fashion, "*Noir.*"

Basil laughed harder as he held Thomas close.

"What?" Thomas acted all innocent and cute. "That's the name. Helps keep me looking sexy."

"It keeps you smelling sexy."

Thomas leaned back and placed his hands against his chest. He widened his eyes and blinked them in a girlish flirty fashion. "You think I'm sexy? Aww...Get outta here," he said, smacking Basil with his fingers.

With another laugh, Basil shook his head. "You're definitely zany."

"It's my charm, darling, all in the charm." Thomas snuggled back up against Basil.

Basil heard the SUV come down the long drive and park. He smiled when Rosemary Wallstatt-Franklin slid out. He knew when she saw him because her face lit up.

Rosemary raced across the grounds. "Basil! You're home!" She threw her arms around Basil's neck.

As Basil rocked back, Thomas prevented him from falling back by acting as a counterbalance. He glanced to the side and whispered 'thanks' to Thomas.

"Anytime I can get my hands on you, big guy, I'm happy," Thomas said in a cheerful tone.

Basil flushed a bit at Thomas' words and turned back to hugging his sister back. "Hey, baby girl, missed you too."

"Dang it, Rosie, don't you see the cane? Sheesh, take care with our big brother. He's taken some hits in life," Sage said in a droll tone. Kaden popped him on the head. "Ow."

Rosemary immediately dropped back to her feet and checked out Basil from head to toe. She lingered on the cane, his slip-on shoes, and a patient Stryker sitting next to him. She lifted her gaze and cupped one of her hands around his face. "Oh, big brother, what happened to you?"

As he raised his hand to take her hand in his bigger one, he moved to kiss the back of it and smiled. "I'm a bit battered, Rosie, but I'm home. Still in one piece, just not all of them my own," he said, trying to make light of it.

This time, Rosemary stepped closer and wrapped her arm around his waist. Their clasped hands held between them.

Basil placed a kiss in her hair.

"Now we're complete," she said.

"Yeah, we're back together." He gave her another kiss and released her. "Introduce me to your family."

Rosie brushed away the happy tears and turned to hold her other hand out toward her husband. He left the SUV, holding a blanketed bundle in his arms. "I know you missed our wedding, Bas, but that's in the past. Anyway, this is my husband, Oliver Franklin, and our newest addition, Colter Niall."

A slow smile curled Basil's lips at the name. "You named him for Daddy."

Rosie nodded with a smile. "Since our oldest is named after Oliver, he insisted a second son carry Daddy's name. This little fella is the last of the bunch though. I had a rough time with him and doc said no more for me."

"I'm sorry, Rosie, I know you wanted half a dozen at least," Basil said. He looked over at Oliver and held out one of his hands.

After he shifted the tiny bundle, Oliver shook hands. "It's good to finally meet you. Thank you for your service. Thankfully, I helped to initially talk her out of the six-pack group of kids. Three are what we can handle."

"Good man," Basil said as the shake turned into a side hug to avoid squishing the sleeping baby. "It's a pleasure to meet the one who captured Rosie's wild heart. I hear you serve too."

"I'm a sergeant with the Kalispell Police Department," Oliver said.

"Oliver is in training to become a detective," Rosie said. "It's so exciting."

"I thought you said you'll miss seeing my ass in uniform," Oliver teased.

Rosie smacked her husband's arm and looked at Basil with a smile. "Would you like to hold Colter?"

"Umm." Basil tilted his head to look at the tiny baby. "I don't know, he's so little and I'm not my best."

"He's not going to break. Babies bounce thanks to all the padding on their butts," Sage said as he moved closer to see their nephew.

"Oh, hush, you," Rosie said and smacked a kiss on Sage's cheek. She scooped her son from his father's arms and laid him in the crook of one of Basil's arms. "Now, support his head like this." She positioned his hands for him. "Can you use your other hand to secure him?"

Basil glanced to the side and found Thomas. "Could you help me?"

"Always." Thomas took Basil's cane and braced his body again Basil.

Basil moved his hand underneath the precious bundle of sleeping baby and blankets. "Oh, wow, he's so light and precious." He breathed in the warm inviting scents of powder, soap, and milk. The combination was something only a baby could offer. He pressed a light kiss to the forehead.

"He'll get bigger. They always do," she said as she adjusted the blanket.

He stared down upon his nephew's tiny face. "Hey, sleepy boy. It's good to meet you," he whispered. "He's beautiful, Rosie." His tone was soft and filled with awe.

"Aww, look at that itty bitty sleepy face," Sage said and cooed in the silliest tone.

"Did you ever hear the saying don't wake a sleeping newborn? This is the time," Kaden said in a low tone as he tickled his partner's side, but leaned in to check out the baby. "Job well done with this one, Rosie. Sorry, Oliver, you did your part too. What was it? One night?"

Oliver snorted at the dig, but smiled back. "He's not our only one, Basil."

"What? There's more?" Basil asked.

The others chuckled.

Rosemary said, "We have two older ones, but there's nothing like having a newborn."

"Including the sleep deprivation," Oliver said and called for the other children. "Ryan, Carrie, come and meet your Uncle Basil. He's your mama's big brother and served as a Marine."

Two kids raced over from the SUV. The boy had his father's coloring. The girl had her father's eyes but the rest of her was all Rosemary. They stood next to Oliver as he placed a hand on their shoulders.

"Basil, I would like to introduce our children. Our son is Oliver Ryan Junior, but we call him Ryan and he's ten. This little beauty is our Carolyn and she's six," Oliver said. "Kids, this is your Uncle Basil."

Basil glanced at Rosie, who nodded at how her daughter carried their mama's name. He looked at Sage, who was leaning into Kaden's hold with a sappy smile. Swallowing, he looked down at the nephew and niece he only read about in Charlie's letters. "Hello, Ryan and Carrie, it's a pleasure to meet both of you and your baby brother."

"You were away for a long time," Carrie said, with the honesty and forthright nature of a child.

"I was very angry with my daddy, your grandpa."

"You're not angry anymore?"

"No, little one, I'm not. I talked with my daddy, even though he's in heaven, I still talked to him and explained things," Basil said.

"Did you fight the bad guys?" Ryan stepped closer, pushing back his kid-size Stetson.

"I did have to fight them. I fought against the ones who attacked America to make sure they don't hurt anyone else."

"Neat! Daddy, did you hear that?" Ryan asked, leaning his head back.

"I did, son," Oliver said with a smile and then at Basil. "He's in the shooting and fighting stage."

"I wanna be a cop like Daddy," Ryan said.

"I remember enjoying that stage myself," Basil said and smiled down at Ryan. "A cop is an awesome thing to become. It's a big responsibility though. My daddy taught me to respect the rifle and who I aimed at every time. You must remember that, Ryan. Always respect the weapon in the hand and what you're aiming at because they also have a heart. Whether it's a bad guy or a deer, they have a heart." His voice thickened with the advice he learned a long time ago.

Thomas tightened his grip just enough to let Basil know he wasn't alone.

With wide eyes, Ryan nodded his head like a wobble doll.

Baby Colter decided to make himself the center of things. He wiggled amongst his blankets and uncle's shaky arms, soft whimpering noises and waved his little fists. His rosebud mouth opened and closed in a suckling motion.

"Uh-oh," Basil said as he looked at his tiny nephew.

"Relax, Basil, he's not going anywhere," Thomas said, guiding his hands. "Little fella is waking up from his nap. It appears he wants his mama soon." He grazed the back of a finger along the soft cheek.

"What's that dreamy look for?"

Glancing over at Basil with a smile, Thomas shrugged and looked back at the baby. He moved his finger around the wisps of dark curls on the small head and touched the little fist when it came near him. "He's beautiful. I always wanted one of them, even when I realized I was gay. It didn't turn me away from the idea of holding my child one day."

"You want to be a father?"

"Yes, but it's one of those down the road type of dreams." Thomas shrugged and cooed when the baby waved his fists as his face darkened. He let out spits and spurts of tiny hungry cries. "Uh-oh. Lemme take him to mama before those cries turn into deafening screams. Take your cane back before I let go of you."

Cautious of the bundle of hungry baby, Basil let Thomas take point at changing their holds. He grabbed hold of his cane as Thomas rocked the baby while he walked over to where Rosie was standing and talking with Lorraine.

Rosie turned to Thomas' call and smiled. "How did you get a hold of him?"

"Couldn't resist and Basil was getting scared," Thomas said.

"Was not," Basil retorted.

With an air kiss over his shoulder at Basil, Thomas continued to rock the baby as the cries grew steadily louder. "We either have a full diaper or somebody is getting hungry."

"Oh dear, I know that sound. This is the combination of both types of cry. I thought he would last a bit longer," Rosemary said as she took hold of her son. "Thomas, could you run to the back of the SUV for the diaper bag?"

"Sure," Thomas said and jogged away to grab the bag. On his way back, he stopped and pointed his finger down next to Basil's side. "I think Stryker wants to play." With a grin, he followed Lorraine and Rosie into the house. The baby's cries getting louder as Rosie predicted.

Basil found the two older kids staring down at Stryker, who whined and wagged his tail. Oliver was barely able to keep the kids in place. He knew how to fix this problem. This part was easy—dogs and kids knew all about each other.

"Ryan, Carrie, this is my best buddy, Stryker. He's a good fella and loves to chase tennis balls. Do you have one?" he asked.

Ryan and Carrie shook their heads.

"It's okay. There's a bucket on the porch. Go get one and have fun. Stryker, go play."

Dog and kids raced away.

"It's not like we don't have a collie waiting at home along with two lazy cats," Oliver said as he kept an eye on the trio.

"There are three working border collies here, but they stay with one of the cowboys. Stryker will be good with them. He'll corral them if they go too far."

"You can't go wrong when kids and dogs are together. They'll race each other around until they collapse," Oliver said and chuckled.

They walked over to the main group and Sage lowered his phone. His eyes saddened from whatever he heard.

"Sage? What's wrong?" Basil asked.

"I talked with the doctors and they don't recommend seeing Mama. She's lucid and in the past still. If she sees us or the kids..." Sage said with a shrug.

"It's upsetting to not see her, but you told me it would be like this. Rosie knows what to expect," Basil said. "Doesn't matter. We're all together."

"We're going to have one helluva barbecue shindig!" Charlie called out as everyone whooped.

♫

As the sun lowered in the western sky, Basil saw a golf cart bustling across the yard. His eyes widened and he walked-limped toward it as the silver-haired lady stepped out and rushed to him. He wrapped his hand around the thin body and lifted her off her feet. He set her down, pressing kisses to her hair.

"Aunt Patti, oh, it's so good to see you," he whispered against her hair. He closed his eyes and breathed in his aunt's warming scent, another anchor to home. His mother's sister was almost the spitting image of her but with greener eyes. When he looked at his aunt, he could see his mother at the same age instead of being lost in her illness and kept from them.

"Oh, my beautiful boy, you returned to us," Patti said as she stepped back and held his face between her hands. "Oh, you're such a sight for these eyes."

"I missed you so much."

"Same here, beautiful boy. A little worn for wear, but you're with us."

"What are you doing here? What about Mama?"

"The evening nurse came over and your mama is sound asleep with the medication. If she wakes, the nurse knows how to calm her. She shooed me away to see my family," Patti said. She smiled and turned to greet Rosemary and Sage as they raced over to her.

"Oh, you're here, I'm so happy you're able to be with us," Sage said.

"Same here, my sweet one." Patti moved to Rosemary. "Where are those beautiful babies of yours, my dear?"

With a laugh, Rosemary led their aunt away to the picnic tables were folks continued to gather and eat. The kids sat at one end, Stryker not far from them as he waited for something to drop. Oliver sat on a nearby chair, rocking the baby and feeding him a bottle. After Patti spent time with the older ones, becoming their grandmother figure, she went to Oliver and the baby. When she held the baby boy, she settled in the chair, to rock him, whispering sweet words to him. All the while, she looked up and spoke with others who welcomed her to the gathering.

Sage hugged Basil out of nowhere and he laughed.

"What's that for?"

"I'm damn happy and feeling great. Oh, look, the band decided to pull out the instruments. Gotta go play," Sage said and raced off.

With another laugh, Basil limped back to a lounge chair and settled his aching body in it. He smiled when Lorraine walked over and slid a couple of pillows behind his back. "Thank you, Lorraine."

"Welcome, my boy. It's good to see your auntie enjoying herself."

"I know. I didn't think she would be able to leave. I'm sure she would love to spend time with you."

Lorraine kissed his temple and left to sit with Patti. Together, they would spoil the little ones with their endless love.

Leaning against the pillows and chair, Basil listened as the band played a few acoustic tunes. Of all people, it was Charlie who asked Josh if he could use his fiddle. Shocked, Josh gave him permission and Charlie went all out. He strummed and plucked right along with the rest of the band, not missing a beat on the fiddle.

While the music quieted down to Simon strumming his mandolin and Randall picking chords on the guitar, Basil enjoyed the evening sounds filled with familiar voices, laughter, and cheers from the children. It was perfect. Another perfect day. He stared at the glass of ice water on the table next to him and grimaced.

"What's that face for? This night has been awesome. No grimaces or frowns allowed," Thomas said as he motioned for Basil to shift to one side.

"There's not much room."

"We'll make room to fit," he said and dropped on the freed spot on the lounger when Basil shifted his legs to one side. "Now, why the long face?"

"Wishing for the ice water to turn into an icy bottle of beer," Basil said.

"Poor baby. No coffee or beer," Thomas teased with a tsk sound.

"Stupid pain meds and my body can't handle it anymore. A single beer makes me sick as all hell and I prefer to not pay homage to the porcelain god if I can help it."

"Don't we all want to avoid that little problem?"

Adjusting his position again, Basil moved his arm. "Come and lean back against me."

"You don't mind."

"I wouldn't offer."

Thomas chuckled at Basil's usual answer to the question. Pulling up his legs to one side, he slid further up, twisted to his side, and snuggled against Basil's chest and side.

Basil secured him close with an arm low around Thomas' waist. He dipped his head and breathed in the soothing scent of this man curled near him.

"It's been a good day," Thomas said.

"Yeah, it has been a good day," Basil agreed.

The loud banging on a chair with drumsticks caught everyone's attention.

Basil saw Kaden and those damn sticks standing next to an empty chair. Kaden shifted his weight a few times and cleared his throat even more.

"He looks nervous. Doesn't he?" Thomas whispered.

"Are you gonna stand there dumb and mute?" Randall called out.

A flush colored Kaden's cheeks, but disappeared. "I wanted to hold things up a moment. If I could have everyone's attention so I can say something." He looked around the scattered group who filled the side lawn and porch. "A while ago, I'd forgotten what it was like to have a loving, supportive family. Until I came back home to White Pine and tracked down my childhood friend. To be honest, I deliberately and obviously stalked him."

"I knew it," Sage crowed.

Kaden shrugged as if to dismiss it. "Once Sage and I got over the bumps in our path, we made some pretty sweet music together. In more ways than one."

"Oh shit, don't spill all of our secrets," Sage said as he rushed over from where he sat. He waved his hands to stop Kaden until Kaden caught both of them. "What are you doing?"

"Sage, you've held my heart since we were boys. Since that moment long ago in our cavern, I was yours. Always," Kaden said.

"Kaden, what are you—" Sage trailed off as his mouth dropped.

Kaden dropped to one knee in front of him. Everyone cheered in raucous tones until Charlie whistled sharp and high to shut them up.

Kaden dug into his pocket and pulled out a small velvet bag. He held the bag out on his palm. "Sage Alastair Wallstatt, you hold all the love in heart. Thanks to the Supreme Court's decision, I can finally ask this question. Would you do me the honor of becoming my husband?"

Sage brought both of his hands to his face and covered it. He nodded several times and lowered his hands. Tears spilled down his face. "Yes. Holy shit, yes, yes, yes," Sage said. He bent forward, held Kaden's face between his hands, and kissed him multiple times in between the yeses.

Everyone cheered loud and boisterous, stomped their feet, and clapped while the couple continued to kiss, oblivious to what was happening around them.

Rising from his position, Kaden poured the contents of the bag into his palm. "These are our engagement rings. You'll help me pick the wedding bands, if we want them, later." He picked up one ring and slid it on Sage's finger. Sage repeated the tender moment with the other ring.

They hugged and kissed one another.

"Woohooo! Congratulations!" Basil shouted from his chair, lifted his hands high above his head and clapped them.

Thomas called out more cheers. He bounced out of the chair and raced over with Josh to hug and give them well wishes. They checked out the bands.

Basil watched the scene unfold. Sage and Kaden went around, accepted hugs and congratulations from everyone, including Patti. He never saw his brother happier than this moment, beaming with love. As he attempted to push forward to climb off the chair, Sage ran over and sat in Thomas' spot.

Instead of rising, Basil embraced his younger brother. "I've never been prouder of you. Congratulations, baby brother. May everything you ever wished for come true. He's a lucky man to have you," he said.

Sage pulled back and brushed the back of his hand against his face to wipe off more tears. "I can't believe he did that." He looked over to find Kaden in the crowd.

Rosemary rushed over and sat down behind Sage. She wrapped her arms around him and crazy rocked them back and forth in her excitement.

Basil laughed at her enthusiasm.

"Oh my God, how wonderful was that? Lemme see. Lemme see the bands," she said as she tugged Sage's hand toward her.

In order to get a look as well, Basil leaned forward to check out the silver band with a rainbow-colored insert. Sage pulled it off to show the engraving on the inside. Basil brought it closer and read *'To the one who holds my heart. K'*.

"This is beautiful, brother," he said and handed the ring over to Rosemary.

Sage took it back and slid it on his finger once more. "I can't believe he did this," he said again, still in shock about the proposal.

"Hey, as he said, the Supreme Court gave us the right to live as any other human in this country. Now you two get all the benefits of a piece of paper that's legal everywhere you go. Which is helpful once you start touring again," Basil said.

Thomas skipped back. Literally, he freaking *skipped*!

Basil stared and chuckled. Sage laughed next to him.

Thomas flicked them off and dropped on the other side of the lounger. "How exciting is this? A wedding. We're gonna have a wedding," he sing-songed. "Oh, I'm so helping to plan this one. Don't think of doing this without me, Sage Wallstatt."

"I wouldn't dare. Don't worry, I'm sure you'll get a turn soon." Sage glanced between him and Basil, who lifted an eyebrow. "I've seen how you two have become closer these last few days. I'm not blind."

Thomas flushed hard. "No pressure, of course, since you know I'm not wrangling for a proposal anytime soon," he assured Basil.

"Of course," Basil said, but wasn't so reassured by the comment or thought.

How could one man go from single and somewhat dating, to possibly enter a promised engagement in one night? Is that even possible?

Basil let his gaze drift away as the others chatted around him.

Thomas returned to his curled-up spot next to Basil. He lifted to whisper in Basil's ear, "Come to my room later tonight. Something I want to show you."

Basil turned to look at Thomas. "What is it?"

"You'll see. If you want to take a chance on life and love, come to my room," Thomas said as he pushed out of the chair and walked off to talk with others again.

Basil tilted his head as he watched Thomas. What did he want with his life? He didn't know.

Chapter Nine

After getting a shower and dressing in soft sweat-pants, Basil limped-walked across the hall. As he was about to knock on the door, he heard a low grunt of masculine need. He tapped his knuckles on the door. "Thomas?"

Come inside and lock the door behind you," Thomas said.

"Either be a git and leave or go inside, Marine," Basil whispered to himself. He opened the door, stepped inside and locked the door as Thomas requested.

The room was dark, lit only by a soft light in the corner and the moonlight streaming through the open blinds and sheer curtain. It revealed a naked Thomas reclining on the bed, one hand jacking his cock.

The sexual image slammed into Basil, almost taking his breath with it. Arousal hit him just as hard as his cock went from being half-mast to full and stiff. The head almost peaked over the edge of the waistband that barely hung around his hipbones.

"Hiya," Thomas said.

"What are you doing?"

"Jacking off and hoping you could help me with this sudden need deep inside," Thomas said.

Basil moved until he stood at the end of the bed. He watched Thomas give him a come-hither smile as he turned on one side, bent one leg up, and revealed the bottom of a thick dildo he shoved deep in his hole. Thomas grasped the bottom with fingertips and twisted it with a groan.

"Naughty boy, you started before me. I don't know if I should help you," Basil said with a teasing smile.

"Aww, come on, I did this for you," Thomas said as he turned and wiggled his ass and dildo at Basil.

Basil crooked his finger. "Crawl down to me."

Thomas crawled slow and steady for when he moved his ass, his eyes almost rolled back with pleasure.

"Is that toy nice and deep inside you? Stretching you out and hitting the right spots," Basil said.

"Oh, yeah, my favorite one," Thomas said as he stopped in front of Basil and knelt. He went to touch his cock, but Basil slapped his fingers.

"Don't touch." Thomas whimpered. "You started this. I'm going to finish. I'm not too flexible, but we can work around it."

"Ooh, a man that takes control. I like to play around with a lover."

Basil gripped Thomas' chin between his fingers of one hand while his other hand wrapped around Thomas' cock. "This is for me and me alone. Don't think about playing with anyone else, Thomas."

Thomas widened his eyes as Basil snapped out his demands and fondled his cock. "I wouldn't dream of being with someone other than you. I don't cheat."

"Good. Just making sure things are clear before we get closer," Basil said as he released Thomas' chin.

"Just the way I like it," Thomas said as he leaned forward to capture Basil's mouth in a series of deep sloppy kisses. His cock, still in Basil's grip, pressed between them.

When Basil pulled back, he slid his thumb over the flared head and slit of Thomas' reddened spongy cock head. He caught droplets of pre-cum and slicked the head with it.

Thomas moaned as he placed his hands on Basil's waist, his fingers gripping the soft cotton as Basil jacked him, slow and steady, then a harsh pump. "Oh, yeah, just like that."

Basil drifted his other hand around Thomas's hip and found the end of the dildo. He grasped the silicone toy's end and pumped it to match the motion he used on Thomas' cock.

"Oh, shit, oh," Thomas said and whimpered incoherent as Basil worked him from both ends.

"Like this, baby, you like having this big cock in your ass," Basil said, leaning his head forward to nip along Thomas' neck and earlobe. "Is this a vibrator?" He tapped the dildo's bottom with his finger.

"Not thi-*is*—" Thomas' voice when high as Basil hit the right spot. He pulled in a few quick breaths, licked his upper lip and finished. "One."

"There are more?"

Thomas nodded.

"We'll have to check them out."

Thomas stared at him. "Not now."

Basil chuckled. "No, not right now, but I believe I have something for you." He nodded down to where his cock poked out of the sweatpants. He let go of the dildo and brought his hand back to Thomas' hip.

"Oooh, a gift for me," Thomas said as he moved to rest on his elbows and knees to keep his butt in the air. He tugged on Basil's pants until they dropped to the floor.

Basil grunted when cool air hit his erection as Thomas released it from the cotton pants. Thomas skimmed his fingers over Basil's cock, a faint touch from the flared deep purple head, the thick shaft with ropes of veins, to the nest of curls and soft sac underneath. When he gripped the shaft and wrapped his mouth around the head, Basil called out his name in pleasure as moist heat surrounded him.

Basil released his grip on the cane and braced his hands on the mattress, trapping Thomas between them. He bent forward to give Thomas more to play with and suck. When he could, he shifted his weight to one hand, reached his other hand out to find the dildo in Thomas' hole. He grasped the end and pumped it at different speeds and depths. He looked down as Thomas sucked on the flared head while his hand plied the shaft and watched his reactions to see when he hit the prostate.

"There. Oh, Bas, there," Thomas said when he released Basil's cock to let out incoherent noises.

"I should make you come on this first."

"No. No, want you inside for first time," Thomas said as he pushed Basil's hand away and knelt upright to face Basil. His lips were wet and swollen from sucking Basil's cock. "I want you inside me."

"Get the lube and condom," Basil said.

"I'm clean. Haven't been with anyone in a year and had the test."

"I've been in rehab hospitals and tested for everything. I'm clean too."

"I only want you, as is, nothing between us," Thomas said as he cupped one hand around Basil's whiskered cheek. He leaned up and pressed several deep kisses against Basil's mouth.

"Get the lube," Basil said after a few more kisses. He slapped Thomas' ass, hearing him *yip* in surprise. "Go. Don't touch that dildo."

Thomas grumbled as he turned and crawled back up the bed. He grabbed a bottle from the nightstand and made his way back. He also dragged a pair of pillows with him. He poured lube in one palm and slicked Basil's entire cock. He capped and tossed the lube aside.

He flopped on his back, adjusted the pillows behind his head and upper back, and let his feet drop until he found the wooden frame of the bed. He opened his legs wide and shifted until his ass hung over the edge. The dildo remained deep inside, stretching his hole.

"Would be easier on your knees," Basil said.

Thomas shook his head. "I want to watch you. Until it hurts you too much, when that happens we'll get into a different position. Okay?"

With a nod, Basil cupped one hand under Thomas' sweet round butt and grasped the dildo with his other fingers. He pulled on it with a slow, twisting fashion to keep up the sensation.

"Shit... Oh..." Thomas gripped the sheets as his back arched while Basil slipped the thick toy out of his hole. "Toss it anywhere."

Knowing they needed to clean it later, Basil dropped it next to the bed. "Wrap a leg around my hip," he said as he positioned his cock at the stretched, relaxed hole. When Thomas did what he asked, he pushed his way in one slick stroke until he lodged himself deep in Thomas. He held still as Thomas' body flexed and adjusted to his girth and length, a little more than the toy.

"Oh, damn, you're thick."

"You're so fucking tight around me," Basil said as he groaned when Thomas' hole gripped his shaft.

"Shit, I feel stuffed with you inside," Thomas said on the edge of a moan. He poked the tip of his tongue out as his eyes closed from the sensations. His body arched and writhed under him while his internal muscles clenched around Basil's cock.

"Are you good?"

"Oh, yeah, move, fuck me hard," Thomas said. "I want to feel you tomorrow." He opened his eyes and stared at Basil. "Fuck me hard, Marine."

With a grin, Basil braced his hands on the mattress edge near Thomas' hips. He rolled his hips, tested his stability and strength to make sure he wouldn't fail his younger lover. He widened his stance a bit and yanked Thomas' ass closer to his thighs as he pulled and snapped hard inside. His sac slapped Thomas' ass.

"Oh, shit," Thomas said. "Do it. Fuck me."

After another adjustment of his hands, leaning toward Thomas and the bed, Basil flexed, snapped, and thrust his hips hard. He drove his cock in and out of Thomas' hole. He fixed his angle and with another push, he knew he pegged Thomas' gland. All words became incoherent as he continued to nudge and hit the gland with every stroke.

He worked both of them until the bed rocked with his movements. Sweat dripped down his spine and chest as he continued to thrust and push into Thomas' warm tight hole. Thomas continued to scream and make those beautiful noises he could get used to hearing.

"Jack yourself. Almost there," he said.

Thomas managed to wrap his fingers around his dick and worked himself.

"Almost there," Basil whispered.

"Same here... Oh..."

Basil clamped his hands on Thomas' hips, dug his fingers into the skin until he may leave bruises, for a few hard fast thrusts. Thomas called out Basil's name as he shot white ropes of cum across his belly and chest. With another quick shove, Basil grunted Thomas' name as he poured himself deep inside Thomas' body.

Exhausted and hurting, he panted and shivered. He managed to slip out of Thomas' body. "Thomas..."

"I have you," Thomas said, his voice a harsh whisper.

Basil let himself collapse in Thomas' sure grip and tender embrace for the rest of the night. His body hummed with pleasure and satisfaction.

In the past couple of weeks since the barbecue, Basil continued to enjoy his nights with Thomas to where he barely slept in his room. They spent all their free time together, but Basil was determined to be useful at the ranch.

He was working in the office, but he couldn't make heads or tails out of the three different styles of organization. Each one created by Sage, Kaden and Charlie. He tapped his fingers on the desk and stared at the troublesome trio sitting on the opposite side. Sage sat all nonchalant, legs stretched out in front of him. None of them squirmed with fear, not even when he pulled out his stern military face. He needed to practice it in the mirror.

Bas waved a hand behind him at the two lateral filing cabinets. "Can one of you show me exactly where all the invoices are kept for the feed?"

With a roll of his eyes, Sage got up and walked around to the cabinets. He pulled one. "It's here under Kellerson Feed." He paused as he ruffled through the folders. "It's not here. Where is it?"

"It's under Feed," Kaden said as he rounded the desk and opened drawer. "Huh. No folder. I labeled it and everything."

"Charlie?" Basil asked.

"Bottom left-hand drawer of your desk. Hanging folder marked Feed," Charlie said. "I'm too damn old to go messing around with the drawers."

Basil opened the drawer and located the folder. He watched his brother and Kaden drop back in the chairs. "Anyone learn this valuable lesson, boys?"

"Too many hands in the pot," Charlie said as he whapped the back of Sage's head.

"Ow. Hey! Why is it always me who gets smacked? He did it too," Sage said as he rubbed his head. He then nodded toward his fiancé. He turned and sneered at Kaden. "I don't like you anymore. Boo. All is off."

"Please don't do the diva act. Leave that to Thomas," Kaden said.

"How many times has he tried to pull that off?" Basil asked.

"Too damn many," Kaden said.

Sage waved his hand again to dismiss the issue and slouched down in the chair. "Back to the freaking filing issue. What do you want to do, big brother?"

"I want all of you to keep your dirty hands out of this office. I'll figure out an organization system that covers everything, even the books for the band. No one else can alter anything once it's finished. If you want to request something, I'll have a box or form or something. I don't know yet. All mail goes through me so I can keep all the invoices and payments in here," Basil said and tapped his fingers on the desk. "Do you know I found three invoices and a very nice check on the entrance table in the hallway this morning?"

"Oops, sorry about that. Got distracted," Kaden said and glared at his fiancé.

Basil smacked his hand on his forehead. "Unbelievable." He adjusted his position in the chair when his back twinged a protest. "New rule in place. Immediately. All mail dropped on this desk first. Do I need to create a sign for everyone to know?"

"Probably would be helpful," Kaden said.

With a sigh and mumble, Basil rolled the chair closer to the laptop. As he reached for the keyboard, his back sent up another protest. This one was deeper and painful. One of his hands curled into a fist at the pain, but he held back a sound.

"Bas? You okay?" Sage asked.

"Yeah. Good," Basil said as he opened a new document, pumped up the font size, and typed the new rule. He sent three copies to the printer. "Kaden, could you get that and post one by every exterior door? Just stick a freaking push pin through it, I don't care how."

"Not a problem," Kaden said.

Basil opened a drawer and pulled out a box of colorful pins. He tossed it over to Kaden, who caught it with ease. He pointed a hand to Kaden and said, "Bring it right—"

"Back, yes, I know," Kaden interrupted with a grin and left the office.

"What else do you need from us?" Charlie asked.

"Don't know. I'm going to have to go through every drawer, file and paper to create a list of what we have. I can't find a detailed report of anything, not even the damn general ledger. Before I touch any numbers, I want to make sure I know where everything belongs around here. I took a couple of online courses, but not much," Basil said.

"Do you want to take a course? There are online courses for bookkeeping and the programs?" Charlie asked.

"I looked and they're a bit expensive."

Sage waved a hand. "Go ahead and order the classes. We'll have it covered with the upcoming sales of the six two-year-olds we trained and ready to hand over to their new riders."

"Are you sure?"

"While things aren't organized, I know we've been in the black for the last three years thanks to the tax returns."

"Taxes. Right, I need those. Where the hell are they?"

"I had them in the lateral file," Sage said and looked at Charlie.

"Last three years are in the right lower desk drawer. The rest are in a box in the closet," Charlie said and pointed to the back of the office and the two doors. "I'll let you two continue this. I have things to do outside."

"Great. I forgot about the closet," Basil said and looked back as Charlie rose and headed to the door. "Thanks for the help, Charlie."

A soft woof stopped Charlie as Stryker woke and raced away from the new bed Basil placed in the corner. He danced around Charlie's feet, eager to do something else.

"Do you mind if he tags along with me?" Charlie asked.

"Not at all, it seems he adopted you."

"I don't mind. He's a smart little fella."

"Let him run with you. I'll be working here the rest of the day," Basil said.

Charlie waved, called to Stryker, and they left.

"One of us can help you with the physical stuff," Sage offered after Charlie left.

"Sage, please, I can manage it."

"I know. You don't want to bring it up, but Bas, please, I can see the winces crossing your face. Plus the skin around your mouth tightens and turns white. You're in pain."

"I'm always in pain. It's a matter of managing it so I can concentrate on moving forward." Bas tightened his fingers into a fist as a sharp spasm went deep in his lower back. "Sonofa—" He bit the mumbled curse. As the pain deepened, he leaned forward and gasped. His vision went fuzzy as the spasms multiplied. Then his back locked up and froze in position. "Fuck, can't move."

"Bas, Basil, what's going on?" Sage asked as he appeared in front of him, kneeling on the floor and holding him in place.

"Spasms. Bad. *Shit.*"

"Where are your pills?"

"Not going to help. Shit, fuck, *shit.*" Basil continued to curse and ended it with a sharp cry of pain, unable to hold it back.

"What the hell is going on in here?" Thomas' voice was a welcome relief to Basil.

When he opened his eyes, Basil watched Thomas push Sage out of the way.

Thomas crouched and finally sat on the floor until they could see one another. "Hey there, I'm here, Basil. Talk to me. What's going on?"

Basil explained the problem in between cries of pain.

"Sage, find Doc Evan *now*. This isn't stopping anytime soon," Thomas ordered.

Sage yanked out his cell phone and dialed. "Doc Evan, Basil's in intense pain. Can you get here?"

Basil lost track of the phone call.

"Squeeze my hand, here, let me help." Thomas placed his hand in Basil's white knuckled grip. He lifted their hands and pressed his lips to Basil's knuckles. "We'll get you through this."

"Hurts like fucking hell," Basil admitted.

"Please tell me this wasn't because of last night. I hate to think what we did hurt you. I never want to hurt you," Thomas said in a lower voice so their words were private.

"No, no, Thomas. What we do is special and can never hurt me. It's my body falling apart, that's all."

"Are you sure?"

"Yes, darling."

Thomas raised his eyebrows. "Darling?"

Basil managed to smile. "You like?"

"Perhaps, as long as I can hear more times and get used to it," Thomas said as he drew his fingers down Basil's cheek.

"I'll make sure of it," Basil said and gasped at another painful spasm. "Damn back locked tight. Can't move."

"It's going to be okay. We'll get you back in working order. Stay put until Doc Evan gets here." Thomas moved his gaze from Basil for a moment. "Sage? What about Doc Evan?"

"He's on his way home and will be here in ten minutes. He said to grab an ice pack from the freezer and apply it to help the swelling. You can take a couple of anti-inflammatory pills. I'll get it," Sage said.

"Do you want the pills?" Thomas asked Basil.

"They don't help, I have too high of a tolerance to over-the-counter stuff." Basil groaned as his back remained locked and the muscles felt like they were contracting and twisting around something. He kept his hand around Thomas' hand, flexing and releasing it.

"Looks like we need to figure out new physiotherapy for you," Thomas said. "I get to put my hands all over you. Woohoo!" He winked and whispered in Basil's ear. "Not that I haven't already."

"Yeah, my stitched and scarred roadmap of skin. Not pleasant."

"Shush, you. I like it."

"I hate it. It's a reminder of everything that happened."

"I got it. Here you go, Basil. I saw the doc pulling into the driveway. He'll be here in a moment," Sage said. "Okay, this is going to be cold. Thomas, help me with his shirt."

Basil felt air on his skin as Thomas raised the shirt. He heard Sage's gasp at the damage.

"Holy crap, Bas," Sage said.

"Not now, please. One problem at a time," Basil pleaded.

"The ice, Sage," Thomas said.

Basil felt them drape a light towel and an ice-cold compress. "Lower to the right."

Thomas adjusted the pack.

"Better."

"Hey, everyone, good thing I was on my way home," Evan said.

Basil was glad to hear the doctor's voice and said, "Thanks for getting here."

"I know you told these two and you're in pain, but can you tell me exactly what is going on and what you're feeling?"

Basil saw another pair of legs stand by Thomas. "Started with a twinge. Then spasms that felt like every muscle and scar is twisting like taffy. Now I'm locked in this damn position and really tired of staring at the carpet," he said.

"I can fix that!" Thomas said in a bright tone. He dropped and flipped on his back, looking up at him upside down. He waved with a big silly smile on his face.

"Knucklehead," Basil said.

"I'm better looking than any old carpet. Even if I'm wrinkling my precious outfit." Thomas flicked his fingers down the pale green Henley.

"How about changing into dusty old jeans and standard T-shirt?"

"Oh, how dare you suggest such a thing? I'm a peacock, good sir, and must keep up appearances." Thomas sent him several air-kisses.

"I do like peacocks. Fabulous birds." Basil chuckled that turned into a groan with another spasm. "Now, Doc. It's happening now on the lower right."

Evan said, "I'm moving the pack and you'll feel my hands. Okay?"

"Most of the surface skin is numb from the scars, doubt I'll feel much except the disorganized and aggravated nerves." He stared down at Thomas who continued to make funny faces at him and grip his hand. He grunted when he felt one dig.

"Felt that?" Evan asked.

"Yeah."

"What was it like?"

"A dig against the twist and bone." Basil answered a few more questions as Evan worked him over. He grunted with pleasure and felt his eyes roll back with relief as the doc performed a deep tissue massage. "Ah, shit, that feels good."

"Hey, there's only one way you make that look for me," Thomas said with a big of a grumpy face. "I need to learn this if I want to see that yummy look again." He rolled to pop back on his feet.

Basil grinned and moaned as the doctor worked his muscles and showed Thomas what to do. When they unlocked his back and helped him to an upright position, he twisted to each side and sighed in relief.

"Better?" Evan asked.

"Yes."

"Let's get you to your room and do a more detailed exam. I may have you visit the clinic for an X-ray. With all this damage, you could be prone to arthritis and I don't want that to aggravate your condition. Thomas, could you join us?" Evan said as he gathered the mess and his bag.

"Wouldn't miss it," Thomas said as he grabbed the cane for Basil.

With Thomas and Evan on either side, Basil managed to get to his feet and wobbled for a few moments. "I'm a little woozy."

"Probably from being bent over for so long," Evan suggested.

In slow movements, they left the office and headed to his room. They helped him back on the bed and Basil groaned. He covered his face with both arms and let out a frustrated sigh and short harsh scream of defeat.

"What's that for?" Thomas asked.

"Years of rehabilitation and surgery and this is where I'm at. It fucking sucks to be confined in this body."

"Hey. You're better off than some. You have all your limbs and mobile. The biggest thing is you're still fucking alive." Thomas smacked the back of his hand on Basil's chest.

Once he lowered his arms, he stared at Thomas. "Still fucking sucks."

"You're a grumpy ass patient," Thomas said and wagged a finger at him.

"Didn't your doctors tell you how you'll need different therapies for the rest of your life? Those third-degree burns damaged your body down through the muscle, Basil. You're lucky it didn't hit your spine and pelvis or it would be worse," Evan said. "Do you want to give up and stay loopy on painkillers?" He held up his hand toward Thomas to stop his protests.

Basil kept his gaze blank.

"I'm not going to help you become addicted to painkillers, no fucking way," Evan said, pointing his finger at Basil to mark the last three words. "No one here is going to bring you booze or drugs. If you want that life, you'll do it somewhere else."

Basil grumbled.

"Well? Am I wasting my time here?"

"Doc, come on," Thomas said.

Evan shook his head once. "He doesn't need a pity party or dependency on crutches. He's a soldier." He turned his attention back to Basil. "Soldiers can handle the truth. Right?"

"Marine, Doc. I'm a Marine, not a soldier—they're Army."

"Semantics." Evan waved away the difference. "The rest of my point. Do you remember that?"

"Yes. Yes. I'm not giving up, just having a moment."

"Well, moment is over, time to begin the hard work," Evan said. "Thomas, are you willing to learn and force him to do this every day, several times a day? There can be no lapse in this physiotherapy."

"Teach me everything," Thomas said.

With another battered soul-deep sigh, Basil got with the program and worked with them to get his body back in some semblance of normalcy. Part of him hoped they never met Daryl or he would never get a break to sleep.

After watching and helping Basil fight his way back from the spasm episode for the last four days, Thomas wanted to do something to cheer him up. At least, something other than what they did together at night. He wanted to get Basil out of the office for something different. He raced to the kitchen and after a quick talk with Lorraine, prepared a special picnic late lunch.

Once he finished, he packed everything in the old-fashioned wicker picnic basket with all the extras they needed. He went to a linen closet and found the picnic blanket, a pair of lanterns, and the small radio and stuffed them in a bag. Since he knew Basil would be uncomfortable on the rocky ground, he would return for multiple outdoor pillows Basil could rest against.

First thing, he carried the small bag and basket outside and looked for Charlie. "Charlie! I need to borrow a Ranger for the afternoon. Which one can I have?" he called out while stepping down from the porch.

Charlie sniffed instead. "What am I smelling?" He tried to lift one side of the basket, but Thomas yanked it out of his reach.

Since he adopted Charlie as his other human, Stryker danced around Thomas' feet, his nose in the air, and begged for a treat.

"No," Thomas said and smacked Charlie's hand. He pointed to the dog and added, "No for you either." Stryker whined and tried the big-eyed pleading gaze. Thomas shook his head. "Not going to work, pup."

"He gave it a good try," Charlie said as he bent over to scratch the pup's ears. "What's that for?"

"Special lunch for Basil and me to share. Now, I need a Ranger," Thomas said as he held out his hand and flicked his fingers in a gimme motion.

With a grumble about being all hungry, Charlie stepped inside the barn and returned with a set of keys and radio. He slapped both of them on Thomas' palm. He pointed to the nearby gray and blue Ranger. "Take that one. Where should I tell the boys to avoid?"

"The small grove on the western creek."

"Hope you can cheer our boy up."

"That's the plan," Thomas said as he carried everything to the Ranger. He placed his things in the back and covered them with a tarp to keep the surprise. "Make sure no one touches that basket, including you and Stryker." With that threat, he raced back inside to the closet to pick up four pillows. He carried them outside and stuffed them under the tarp. "Same rules apply!"

Charlie laughed.

Thomas ran back up the stairs and through the house. He paused to catch his breath outside the office where Basil spent a couple of hours at a time in between his therapies and walks. He pressed a hand to his chest.

"Sheesh, peacock, you need to get some exercise," Thomas mumbled to himself. He cleared his throat and straightened to fix his outfit and hair after the exercise. When he was presentable, he knocked on the door, stepped inside and walked to the desk. He bent over, with his ass pointing in the air all cute and begging, and braced himself on his elbows. He blinked in a playful, flirty fashion.

"What are you up to?" Basil asked with a smile.

"Are you at a stopping point?"

Basil checked his watch. "It's not time for another round."

"This is something special. Can you stop?"

Basil shrugged. "Sure."

"Good, come with me," Thomas said as he straightened and held out his hand.

Basil moved close enough to clasp their hands together. "Where are we going?"

"Right now, we're going outside and getting in a Ranger. After that is a surprise. Wait..." Thomas stopped and looked around. "Where's your hat or sunglasses?"

"Sunglasses are in my bedroom on the dresser along with the hat."

"Stay here and don't move," Thomas said and went to their bedrooms. He grabbed both of their sunglasses and returned to Basil's side. "Don't want to squint and get a headache. It's pretty warm and sunny outside."

"No, that would just ruin everything."

"See, you get it. Why don't the others?" Thomas kept up the cheerful babble while he helped Basil outside, down the porch's steps and across the yard to the Ranger. He assisted Basil to climb into the seat. "All good?" He handed Basil his sunglasses.

With a flick of his wrist to open the frames, Basil slid them up his nose and nodded. "Good. Damn. Something smells good." He sniffed and looked around. "What am I smelling?"

"A surprise," Thomas said as he ran around, checked under the tarp and climbed in the driver's side. He got his sunglasses in place first. Then he tugged the key from his pocket and inserted it.

With a flick of a few things, he drove away from the house and barns. He kept his hands on the wheel to control the bounciness of the Ranger and not aggravate Basil's pain. A glance to the side and he smiled. Basil leaned his head back and enjoyed the sunshine and gentle wind against his face.

When they reached the creek that broke off from the main northern river, he turned left and followed it down and away from the main grazing lands.

"Are you following the creek?" Basil asked.

"There's a place down here a bit that I fell in love with and visit often when things get rough or crazy. It's quiet and peaceful. You're going to love it."

"I'm sure I'll enjoy everything you planned."

With a quick smile and air kiss, Thomas followed the path broken into the ground. Soon he saw the small grove of trees gathered around the drop and bend in the creek. The change in the water flow created a small waterfall and natural pool before winding through the land once more. A grove of small oaks and pines grew in a semi-circle as if planned by nature to create a serene setting for a picnic. He parked off to the side, but closer enough for Basil.

Thomas climbed out and held his hand to stop Basil. "Wait a moment and let me set up."

He pulled out the bag first and went to the flat area. Within a few minutes, he set up the blanket, radio, and lanterns. He returned to grab the pillows and tossed them in a pile. One more trip to retrieve the picnic basket and motioned for Basil to follow him.

"I take it the pillows are for me," Basil said.

"Yep. Kick off your shoes and go recline against them. We'll adjust them as you need to keep comfortable." Thomas toed off his shoes and walk over the blanket.

Basil stepped out of his sandals and followed. He tried to sit and grumbled.

"Hold up a moment," Thomas said and set down the basket. He hurried over to help Basil bend his body enough to reach the blanket. He tugged and arranged the pillows. "Okay?"

"Yeah, give me a moment." Basil blew out a few breaths as the skin around his mouth whitened. He set the cane aside.

"Oh damn, I'm so sorry. I didn't want to cause—"

"Thomas, stop. Don't treat me like an invalid. Let's enjoy this surprise you created," Basil interrupted.

To hold back another protest, Thomas bit the inside of his cheek. He lowered to his knees, sitting back on his heels.

"I'm good. I promise." Basil gave him a smile and snatched Thomas' hand for a quick kiss to his palm. "Now. What did you make for me?"

"It's a special lunch. I wanted to get you outside under the sun. Other than your walks and nights in the rocker on the porch, you don't get out much."

"I can't wait to see what you made. How did you get such skills in the kitchen?"

"Lorraine. I stole all of her secrets and techniques." Thomas blew and brushed his knuckles against his shirt, spread them out, and stared at his fingertips.

Basil laughed.

As he tugged the basket closer to his side, Thomas unlatched and open the top. He set up the plates, cloth napkins, utensils, and cups. He handed a Thermos jug to Basil to pour. "Sweet tea."

"Thanks, need something cold," Basil said and set to his task.

Thomas pulled out the different containers and bag of thick-cut potato chips. He placed half of a panini on their plates, added a generous spoonful of both the cold pasta salad and green bean salad. After he poured the chips into a bowl and set them within reach, he returned all the extras back in the basket.

"Okay. This isn't a simple fried chicken and potato salad picnic lunch. I'm impressed," Basil said. "What are we going to enjoy?"

"Have to keep you on your toes." Thomas smiled and pointed around the dish. "This is a pesto chicken panini with sun-dried tomatoes and provolone on a ciabatta roll. Then we have a lemony pasta salad with cherry tomatoes, basil and mozzarella. I finished the dish with a green bean salad with tarragon and bacon. Chips are in the middle. Dessert is waiting for later."

"Did you make all of this for us?"

"The basic salads were already built for lunch, but I changed around the dressings and added some extra stuff. The paninis were made fresh from last night's roasted chickens. The dessert was easy to put together. I cheated though and used a bag of potato chips."

"This looks delicious. Thank you for doing all this." Basil scooped up his setting and set it on his lap for easier reach.

Thomas shifted into a different position on the blanket, but stayed close.

While they ate, simple conversation drifted back about favorites, dreams, changes, and anything else they could think about. In spite of some differences, they enjoyed a lot of the same things ranging from movies, books and even certain video games. Laughter and smiles moved between them, neither one noticing how the sun sank deeper other than for Thomas to turn on both lanterns for a soft glow.

Thomas curled closer to Basil. He shared the soft triple-chocolate brownies between them, enjoying the noises of pleasure Basil made while eating the food he made.

As the night grew longer, Thomas lifted his face as Basil tilted closer and their lips met in the sweetest of kisses. Kisses that turned into deeper, melding ones as they learned what each other enjoyed.

His Marine was one hell of a kisser.

Chapter Twelve

The weeks after the wonderful picnic seem to only get better. Sure Basil continued to struggle with his body, but he was used to that problem. His personal life...

Well, things were changing. He and Thomas spent more time together. Thomas even helped around the office, doing things Basil couldn't, while they organized everything. Thomas brought Basil into the kitchen during prep and taught him how to do basic skills. Basil was sure he got in the way more than he helped, but Thomas and Lorraine never kicked him out or got frustrated.

They cuddled on the sofa and enjoyed movie time with the others in the house. It soon became a special night where they had popcorn.

Their personal nights got even better between them.

He was drifting off to sleep when he felt Thomas work soft kisses and nibbles down his chest. He opened one eye and looked down. "Whatcha doing?" His tone was sleepy and thick.

Thomas lifted his mouth from Basil's chest and rested his chin on one pectoral muscle. "Wanna try something different. Do you trust me?"

"Sure."

With a smile, Thomas shifted in the bed and helped Basil prop himself up on several pillows. He kissed and moved across Basil's body, finding all the sensual spots that drove him crazy. He kept moving when Basil tried to hold him. "Nope. Keep your hands to yourself. Tonight, I'm doing all the work."

"Come on. I wanna touch," Basil whined with a smile and plea.

"Nope. You're all mine at my *control*," Thomas said, accenting the last word which they tossed between each other. He planted a harder kiss on Basil, slid his tongue inside so Basil could suck on the tip. He teased Basil's tongue back to give the same pleasure. They claimed one another with tongues, lips, teeth and Thomas' fingers digging into Basil's hair.

Basil lost track of everything as Thomas touched every bit of skin he could, bringing up dark spots on his skin to mark his claim. He opened his legs wider when Thomas touched him. Thomas flicked his tongue over Basil's balls. These bits of torture caused Basil to grip the sheets while he pleaded and begged for more.

After teasing everything down there but his cock, Basil groaned hard when Thomas finally reached his dick. Not bothering with more foreplay, Thomas swallowed him to the root. He gripped the sheets when Thomas bobbed, licked around the crown and that sweet spot underneath. He bit on a scream when Thomas swallowed him again.

"Ah, fuck." Basil made incoherent noises as Thomas worked his cock, licking the pre-cum from the slit and the entire shaft.

Thomas lifted his head, his mouth slick and swollen from sucking Basil's cock. "Want more?"

"Yes. Shit, yes."

Thomas released Basil's cock and patted it when it curled toward Basil's stomach, thick and hard. He stretched and reached behind Basil to grab something. He sat back on his heels and held a bottle of lube. "I'm clean."

Basil licked his lips at what the lube could mean. "Same here."

"Nothing is holding us back."

"There's always my flexibility issue which sucks. It's buggered and fussed around with some of our nights."

"I can handle that part." Thomas stuffed an extra pillow behind him and leaned back with his cock and ass facing Basil. He jacked his cock between two fingers, working it nice and slow. He drew his legs up and back to put his hole on display. "Do you like watching me?"

"Umm..." Basil lost all of his words, but moaned in approval of the show.

Thomas poured lube on his fingers and rubbed them together until well-greased. He trailed his hand under one leg, then his balls and around his rim. He stuck two fingers straight inside him and moaned at the instant stretch. His hips lifted with the sensation as he worked and stretched his hole. He moved his thigh higher to get a deeper twist and pump of his fingers.

"Shit. Fuck. Thomas." Basil strained to not touch him and help with the sensual scene laid out in front of him.

With a moan, Thomas pulled his fingers free and crawled back to Basil. He grabbed the lube and greased Basil's cock until it was shiny. He tossed the bottle aside and straddled Basil's hips. "Ready for me?"

Basil glanced down at his cock that stood ready with a steady amount of pre-cum across his abs. "Please. Come on."

Thomas rubbed his ass against Basil's dick, playing with him, but didn't let him enter. "Do you really want it? This is my favorite way to make love with you. I do want to ride my Marine."

"Please, oh, shit, yes. Take a ride."

Thomas positioned Basil's dick and sank down. Inch by inch, Basil watched his cock disappear inside Thomas. It was fucking exquisite feeling. The tightness and heat around every inch of his cock as Thomas squeezed him inside his body. Thomas bobbed a couple of times, working his rim, and pressed down until his ass met Basil's thighs and balls. He held still, his eyes closed, his body not moving except for his hole as it worked and loosened around Basil.

"Oh my fucking God," Basil said on the edge of a long groan.

When he opened his eyes, Thomas licked his lower lip in a teasing playful style. "You ready for more."

"Do what you want to me, I'm at your mercy. Oh, shit, you feel so fucking tight around me."

"Hmm, same here, Marine." Thomas rolled his hips in multiple ways and his sounds changed when Basil's cock put pressure against the gland. "There. Oh, yes." He lifted and rode Basil's cock. He leaned forward, moving his weight on his hands and hips as he worked Basil's cock. His gaze never left Basil's face, who watched every nuance and emotion cross Thomas' face.

Basil kept a stream of babbles, noises and begging. He tried to thrust his hips up to meet Thomas' downward push, but couldn't get the power he needed.

They became a heady sweaty mess as Thomas continued his ride.

"Oh, shit, you there. I'm so fucking there. Come on me," Basil said.

"Jack me," Thomas said as he captured Basil's mouth for kisses as he rocked his hips harder on Basil's cock. His breathing changed as his gland was hit and pressed. "Please. Jack me off."

Basil slid a hand between them, wrapped his fingers around Thomas' cock and stroked him ever closer to the edge. He ran his thumb along the slit, spreading the pre-cum all over. "Oh, fuck, I can feel you squeeze hard around me when I do this." He worked Thomas' cock faster.

Thomas sped and deepened his rocking, moaning and pleading.

Everything continued to build stronger and harder.

"Oh, there, now. Now." Thomas clamped his ass around Basil's cock and blow streams of cum across Basil's chest.

Basil let his body shudder as he rode the sensations and spurt deep inside Thomas, hearing him cry out as he flooded him. They rode out the orgasms, milking every hot dirty drop out of them, until Thomas collapsed across Basil's chest.

His best fucking night rolled into the worse day of his life. As he laughed and teased Thomas on the porch, Sage and Kaden laughing next to them, Basil saw Evan and the elder Doc Sampson driving across the ranch in their aunt's golf cart.

"Oh, shit." The tone in his voice stopped everyone. "Sage, call Rose. Now."

Sage dialed as Basil spoke and told Rose to become a speed demon and get to the ranch. He hung up and clung to Kaden.

The doctors reached them.

"Boys, I'm sorry," Doc Sampson said as he cleared his throat several times.

"It's time," Basil said.

"Best come with us. Rosemary?"

"On her way," Sage said.

"I'll wait for her. Go with Basil," Kaden said and kissed Sage.

Basil looked at Thomas.

"I'll stay with Kaden. This is family. We'll follow along with Rosemary," Thomas said as he slid his fingers through Basil's hair and kissed him slow and sweet. He met Basil's gaze. "Tell her you fell in love with someone. Tell her your heart is safe."

Basil tugged both of Thomas' hands down and cupped them between his larger ones. He kissed them and then Thomas' lips. He pulled away and rose from the chair. He nodded to Sage, who helped him down the steps.

They all got in the golf cart. Doc Sampson drove them back to the small cabin tucked away from the house. Basil took his brother's hand, keeping them together as they faced the inevitable.

When the cottage came in view, Aunt Patti waited on the porch. She embraced each one of them, kissing their cheeks and whispering words of encouragement and love. She took their hands and led them inside the two-bedroom log cabin their parents lived in while they worked on the main house. His mother returned to this cabin, lost in her illness and memories after their father passed. She never left it again.

Instead of the old iron bed, their mother rested on a hospital bed, all kinds of equipment around to support her frail body. Aunt Patti adjusted the homemade patchwork quilt as they drew closer.

"Carrie, can you wake up? Your boys are here," she whispered.

Sage leaned against Basil's side and he wrapped his arm around his brother to hold him close. They both prayed for some hint of recognition.

Over an hour passed with nothing, but it was enough time for Rosemary to rush inside the cabin and join them. Basil saw Sage was about to tease her, but stopped himself. Rosemary moved to Sage's other side. Though neither one spoke to another, they kept their youngest sibling in the middle. She kissed both of their cheeks and their aunt's. "Anything?" she whispered and Basil shook his head.

They waited longer than they thought for their mother to open her eyes. All of her motions weakened and strained.

"Carrie, look, your children are here," Patti said and motioned for them to step closer in her view.

Their mother's eyes were no longer bright and clear like her younger years. Time and cancer took their toll upon her entire body. The coloring remained the same as Rosemary and Sage's hazel green. The gaze stopped upon Basil.

"Niall," she whispered and wiggled her fingers.

Basil took her hand. He bent and kissed the wrinkled spotted skin. "I'm here, Mama," he whispered.

"So like Niall," she said and looked to the others. "Babies...Mine...Sweet ones."

"Mama, we love you," Rosemary said as she hugged Sage against her.

"Love you always, Mama," Sage said.

Their mother returned her gaze to Basil. "So strong. Like Niall. I go to him. He comes home."

"I know, Mama," Basil said and kissed her hand again. He held back the thickness and pain in his voice. "It's time for you to sleep and find him walking through the door."

With a soft smile, Carolyn Wallstatt closed her eyes and slipped away from them. Doc Sampson moved around to turn off the machines.

Patti, Basil and the others gathered around the bed. Hugging and crying, they clung to one another in the aftermath of the loss.

2 Weeks Later

After saying the final goodbyes to their mother, sending her off to find their father, Basil knew there was one more goodbye he had to make. He needed to do this to feel free to move forward and love Thomas with his whole heart and soul. This was the final piece and it was time.

Thomas remained by his side the entire trip, never leaving him alone and afraid of what he would face.

It took another three days of planning and traveling, but Basil stood in Arlington National Cemetery. He looked around the peaceful beautiful grounds where so many soldiers, sailors, airmen and Marines slept. There were two different funerals happening. One had full military honors with an escort platoon and a caparisoned horse following the caisson bearing a flag covered casket. Basil saluted as the American flag passed. He released the salute when the procession continued to the gravesite.

Thomas tilted his body toward Basil's side, leaned in close but didn't give him his weight. He kept his voice soft as he said, "Such a solemn exquisite parade. I never saw this before except on television. What is the riderless horse called?"

"He's called a caparisoned horse."

"What does he represent? And the boots. Why are the boots reversed in the stirrups?"

"The tradition dates back to Roman times or even older and only for the high-ranking fallen soldiers. The boots symbolize that the fallen won't ride again and the missing rider is looking back on his family one last time. It's one of the most honored traditions for a fallen soldier or Marine. The six black horses lead the caisson."

"Their harnesses jangling and the rumble by the wheels are unreal."

"Everything is done in formation and precision. The Caisson Platoon is known as the Old Guard. They train and meticulously prepare each horse and themselves for every funeral. Once they reach the burial site, the casket carried by the guard, and the platoon leaves to make ready for another funeral. It's an honored responsibility from escorting all military personnel to their final resting places and protecting them. Do you remember the eternal flame at Kennedy's tomb and the unknown soldiers?"

"They watch over those as well."

"Yes, it's the same guard."

"Would you have it?"

"No, I left with a medical discharge as a non-commissioned officer, a sergeant. I'll receive the basic honors though if I chose to be buried here with others I served."

"What about Larry?"

"As befitting all soldiers and Marines who die in the line of duty, they received full honors. He would have been one of them. I couldn't leave the hospital to pay him respects and when they buried him."

"Is this your first visit?"

"Yes."

"Then it's time for us to find your partner's final resting place." Thomas took Basil's hand in his. He held a simple bouquet of flowers in his other hand.

Basil checked the map he held along with the cane and pointed out the direction. "All military personnel from the Global War on Terror are buried in section sixty."

"Can you make it that far?"

"I'm determined to walk there on my own power."

Though it took some time and a few breaks for Basil to rest on a bench, they reached the section and located Larry's grave, tucked amongst other soldiers from their platoon. He nodded down to the white marble.

Thomas read aloud, "Lawrence James Corbin, Sergeant, USMC." With a bend, Thomas placed the flowers in front of the simple headstone matching the countless others.

Basil stepped closer and placed his hand on top of the marble. He moved one hand back to his pocket and pulled out a quarter, pressed a kiss to the shiny surface, and placed it on the headstone.

"What's that for?" Thomas asked in a soft tone.

"Coins are left for multiple reasons, but mainly to show others someone visited a grave. Those are mostly Lincoln pennies. A nickel would mean the visitor trained with the deceased in boot camp. A dime means they served with the deceased in some capacity. A quarter signifies you were with the deceased when they were killed."

"So that's why pennies are everywhere," Thomas said and looked around. He returned his gaze to Basil, squeezed his hand, and smiled. "Go on and talk to him."

With a lick to his upper lip to soothe his jangled nerves, Basil stared at the grave. "Hey, Larry, I'm sorry I didn't get here sooner to talk to you. Had some issues to work through, but you know all about that." He reached back into his pocket and removed one of the medals he received after the helicopter accident. "Could you believe they gave me all of this metal? For what? A stupid helicopter fell out of the sky and we were stuck inside it. As if we wanted to be there." He shook his head. "You deserve this as much as I do, my love. You saved my ass more times than I could count with your sharp eyes and quick temper. I don't know how I got through everything if we hadn't met in Scout Sniper School. There's so much to tell you, I don't know where to start."

He rubbed his thumb over the cool metal as he talked, needing a touchstone of some sort as he spoke to his lost love of everything that happened since the accident. Tears fell from his eyes, but he didn't bother to hold them back. Not for Larry. He deserved every single tear to fall on his stone. As he finished the quiet conversation, he nestled the medal amongst the flowers, Thomas helped him to bend over and straighten.

With another glance at Thomas, Basil squeezed their hands one more time and released his grip. "There's one more thing, buddy, I hope you would give me permission to move on with my life and love another. You don't have to worry about me anymore though. I promise things are better for me since I returned home. My heart is in very strong hands." Basil glanced at Thomas and smiled. "I found someone to love again and loves me back. Scars, disabilities and all. I wanted to introduce him to you, okay? I know you're smiling down, pleased as hell I moved back to the light."

Basil knew it was time to jump in with both feet. He turned to Thomas. He moved his fingers into a different pocket and found the small bag. He held out his other hand out and Thomas took it once again. "Larry, I would like to introduce my partner, Thomas Bellamy, who brought me out of the darkness. There's one more thing I would like to do." He kissed Thomas' knuckles and hoped Larry would give his permission for moving forward in his life. "As we stand together in front of Larry's stone in this honored land—" He pulled the small bag from his pocket. He poured the two shiny platinum bands into their cupped palms. "Would you do me the honor of becoming my husband, Thomas Bellamy?"

Thomas' eyes widened as he starred at the rings sparkling under the sunshine. Thomas moved his gaze from the bands, to Larry's stone, and up to Basil's. His eyes were watery. He nodded. "Yes, yes, oh, yes," he said, lifting on his toes and pressed their lips together.

The kiss went on for a few more heartbeats until they parted with smiles. Basil slid one band onto Thomas' finger and handed the other to Thomas.

"Forever more will you be mine," Thomas said as he placed the platinum circle on Basil's finger.

Basil clasped their hands together and kissed their knuckles. "Larry, let me introduce my fiancé to you." He smiled at his ring gracing Thomas' slender finger. "Thomas, this is Lawrence, but he would kick your ass if you called him that."

Thomas gave a watery chuckle and looked at the stone. He reached in his pocket and pulled out a few coins. He released Basil's hands and sifted through the pennies until he found one with a Lincoln. "There we go." He returned the rest of the coins to his pocket. He placed the penny on top of the headstone.

"Thank you," Basil said.

With a nod, Thomas looked at the stone. "It's an honor to meet you, Larry." He crouched down and traced the engraving with his fingers. "I promise Basil's heart and love are safe in my strong hands. I won't let you down." He rose and lifted on his toes to kiss Basil's cheek. "Ready to go?"

Basil nodded. "Sorry, Larry, time for us to go. Boss man here wants me off my feet to rest. We'll come back when we can," he said and kissed his fingers and pressed them to the stone. "It's never a full goodbye. Not with you. Sleep well, my love."

Thomas slid his arm around Basil's waist and supported him as they walked away from the grave of Basil's first love.

The last lingering weights and darkness around his shoulders disappeared.

The End

Dreamy...Sensual...Forever Love

A quiet one, Nicole Dennis is the penname of an asexual author of different genres of fiction – both LGBT+ and hetero. Lots of characters, worlds, and stories build up in her head until she must get them down on the screen – anything from romance to fantasy to paranormal.

During the day, she works in a quiet office in Central Florida, where she makes her home, and enjoys the down time to slip into her imagination. She is owned by a feline companion – a fluffy house panther, known as Midnight the Void. A very special furbaby who is FIV+ and polydactyl on her front paws (fluffy danger mittens!).

Website: http://nicoledennis.net
Email: nicoledennis.author@gmail.com
Facebook:

Main: www.facebook.com/NicoleDennis.Author
Page: https://www.facebook.com/NicoleDennis.Musings/
Group: https://www.facebook.com/groups/nicoledennis.author/

Amazon: https://www.amazon.com/author/nicoledennis
Threads: https://www.threads.net/@ndennis_author
Mastodon: https://mastodon.lol/@nicoledennis
QueeRomance: https://www.queeromanceink.com/mbm-book-author/nicole-dennis/
Goodreads: http://www.goodreads.com/author/show/2791975.Nicole_Dennis

Pride Publishing
Southern Charm Series

1 – Rules of the Chef
2 – By the Numbers
3 – On the Green
4 – When in Bloom
5 – Following the Law
6 – According to Design
7 – Unexpected in the End (Coming 2025)
Freebies available on my website or email for PDF

Mischief Corner Books:
Secrets & Silk
Siren Publishing: (BookStrand.com)
Grant's Mechanic (MM)
Unholy Angel (MF Erotic Paranormal)
Fire Jaguars (MMF Paranormal)

1 – Fire Moon Dance
2 – Luna Moon Dance
3 – Dark Moon Dance
Other books are in the works

FatCat Books Ink (Self-Pub home):
New Stories:
Lyon Lynx Clan

Paws in the Snow (Prequel)

McShayne Bloodline

1 – McShayne's Dragon
2 – McShayne's Fae
3 – McShayne's Elf
4 – McShayne's Merman (Coming 2025)

Cheimon Tales

1 – Cracks in the Ice
2 – Strike's Stand (In the works)
3 – Mistletoe's Story (In the works)

Carnival of Mysteries (Multi-Author Collection)

1 – Dryad on Fire
2 – Flames of the Arcane

Re-Releases:
Walk Me Trilogy

1 – Walk Me Down the Middle
2 – Walk Me Through the Haze
3 – Walk Me Through the Darkness

7 Days of Christmas
Built Piece by Piece
At the Masquerade